T0195927

Risk Management Services

John Ball rms

in

Otoys

by C. R. Bryan

Galahand ✲ Press

Order this book online at www.trafford.com
or email orders@trafford.com

Most Trafford titles are also available at major online book retailers.

Print information available on the last page.

ISBN: 978-1-4907-6698-0 (sc)
ISBN: 978-1-4907-6700-0 (hc)
ISBN: 978-1-4907-6699-7 (e)

Library of Congress Control Number: 2015957312

Trafford rev. 11/11/2015

North America & international
toll-free: 1 888 232 4444 (USA & Canada)
fax: 812 355 4082

THIS IS A WORK OF FICTION. ANY RESEMBLANCE TO PERSONS LIVING OR DEAD IS PURELY COINCIDENTAL AND UNINTENDED. ALL LOCATIONS AND ACTIONS ARE FICTIONAL AND TO BE TAKEN AS PURELY FOR ENTERTAINMENT PURPOSES. RISK MANAGEMENT SERVICES IS A FICTIONAL ENTITY AND JOHN BALL DOES NOT EXIST EXCEPT IN IMAGINATION.

However, the problems explored in this story are real. Children should not be forced to labor nor should any persons be used in slavery. And owners, directors and operatives of for-profit entities should not be able to operate with legal protection from corrupt officials.

CHAPTER I

THE TOY FACTORY

The well-dressed Chinese factory representative confidently escorts a group of financiers into a very modern-looking building in northern China. Among the attendees is one who is less smiling and more alert. His name is not the one on the lapel card, for he is there in place of the person who formerly used that name. One who has no use for name tags now.

The representative efficiently escorts his audience through clean and well-organized front offices populated by cheerful, smiling workers. The workers pay strict attention to their computers, only slightly noticing the clutch of foreigners passing through.

"As you can see, this facility is most modern and efficient. We fulfill all our contracts with Otoys on time and below cost. Our workers are among the best-paid in China, and..."

As the rep continues leading the group, John Ball separates from the others, looks carefully around, and then sneaks through a door marked "No Entry" in Chinese and English.

John speeds down several hallways. He emerges into a grimy factory room. It seems endless, a vast area checkered with noisy machines placed at regular intervals on wet and grimy floors stretching into a dark and hazy infinity.

Children are shackled to machines, working to make toys. John signals quiet and begins to force locks open as he passes.

A factory guard removes a dead child from shackles and puts a new child in the shackles. As the guard drags the body away, John rises, snaps the guard's neck, takes the keys, unlocks shackles of several children, cautioning them to silence in Chinese. John moves furtively from machine to machine, whispering in Chinese to the waifs shackled in place. He hands the keys to three children and gestures for them to release the others.

"Here. Take the keys and unlock all the locks. Then run. Do you understand?"

The children nod and begin to free their compatriots. John hears Guards coming to find him. He waits.

Security personnel enter the factory floor and discover the dead guard. They shout for reinforcements and then fan out in the room.

John ambushes three men and downs them. He takes their keys and weapons. He tosses the keys to some other children They nod and scurry away to set their comrades free.

John rushes a door, breaking through rotten wood and wires. Children follow. They are scared and excited. Some have difficulty keeping up with the others. When they are outside, they shade their eyes and look for a direction. They run toward a ravine which leads toward some low hills. More and more children emerge from the hole in the wall of the shiny building. Their line of escape resembles a trail of ants.

John mounts a hill outside the factory. He uncovers a dirty and battered vehicle. He scans for enemies. He gets a pair of binoculars from a bag in the vehicle. He crouches low to avoid being seen.

John uses the binoculars to watch the scene at the factory. The last children are running from the building. Guards run after them. Limousines are leaving with dignitaries. Office workers run from the front. When the people seem to have cleared the building, John uses a device to explode the structure. He smiles faintly.

John leaps into his disreputable utility vehicle and speeds north toward Mongolia. As he drives, he changes his costume and appearance, making himself over into a tribesman. A cloud of dust rises behind his whining vehicle.

Now seeming to be a local tribesman, John Ball takes a wild ride down an almost vertical cliff into a desert canyon full of dry brush. The vehicle splashes through one of the muddy wallows in the bed of an intermittent stream. A lost goat scampers away from the menace.

Behind him he can see there is a pursuit. He scans the skies, expecting aerial assault. He finds a narrow canyon and drives the circuitous bottom, pausing in an overhung bend to complete his disguise. He gathers brush and piles it in the vehicle. Then he drives calmly onward.

An airplane spots him. The airplane circles and fires cannon into the canyon.

"Alright. Have it your way."

John drives up out of the canyon and watches the aircraft circle to begin an attack. John uncovers a rocket launcher and shoots down the airplane. Then he drives fast and recklessly onward. A column of vehicles raises a cloud of dust behind him. He finds some spike chain in a box and tosses pieces of the tire-killer chain behind him. He also scatters spike trapezoids to right and left.

John pulls out a jug of Kvass and drinks heartily. He splashes the smelly beverage on his clothes and on the seat of his vehicle. He produces a sliver of tough dried meat and begins chewing. The pursuers fall behind and their cloud of dust settles as John makes his ugly vehicle move surprisingly fast. In a while, he reduces his speed to a normal pace for a local vehicle.

Day becomes twilight as John slowly drives between scattered yurts on the great Mongolian plain.

He comes to a stop among Mongolian sheepherders. John greets them and raises his bottle of Kvass. The men gather, ready to jest with the rich stranger.

A sheepherder addresses John in Mongolian.

"Hello, stranger. What is happening?"

John replies in Mongolian, "My friends, the idiot Han are shooting at sheep with their airplanes!"

Another herdsman laughs and says, "As always. Did they shoot your beer, also?"

The other herdsmen laugh and relax.

"The gods still laugh in their full bellies. Will you share a cup of my second wife's Kvass?"

Another man says, "If you share your second wife!"

Amidst general laughter. John gets out of the vehicle and shares the beverage among his new friends.

John trades scarves with the men. He reenters his vehicle.

"I go to Ulan Bator to drink what my wife won't give me! Who would come with me?"

The first herdsman and third herdsman toss out the brush and get in the vehicle. They urge motion. John speeds away.

John leads a song.

"Chengis horse was tired that day, but Chengis would not pause…"

The Herdsmen join the song, "Many leagues lay between Chengis and the enemy…"

CHAPTER II

ESCAPE

In a smoky bar and brothel in Ulan Bator the smoke swirls as the doors protest their opening. John leads his rowdies into the bar. He shakes his head side to side, gives a gruff cough and orders drinks, food and entertainment.

Some men leave and some enter. Prostitutes approach the new customers.

John grimaces at his companions and sticks out his tongue. He reaches out for one woman.

"This is the drink my wife number two will not serve!"

The prostitute asks, "Are you an important man, lover?"

John says, "I have something big and important for you."

The other herdsmen engage in similar conversations. John sticks a coin on the forehead of the prostitute and laughs. He flips coins to his friends, who are bemused by this good fortune.

A barfly in awful smelly rags demands, "You might as well give me some of that money, friend."

The barfly takes the coin from the Prostitute and snarls at John.

John laughs at the barfly and calmly stands to confront him.

"You must be a woman! You are the ugliest woman I have ever seen!"

Thugs enter the bar and converge on John. They push through the crowd.

The barfly growls, "You will be a woman soon!" Then he throws a punch and slashes with a knife.

John parries, connects with a punch and ducks beneath the general brawl which ensues.

"Get him! Kill the rich bastard! He's my prize!" The thugs yell.

John escapes, pulling the prostitute with him.

Outside it is a dark night on a dark street in Ulan Bator.

John gives the prostitute a kiss and a handful of coins. He jumps into his vehicle and speeds away. The other prostitutes emerge from the brawl and fight for the coins.

John drives until he comes to a lonely snowy plain with blowing wind. Not a gentle wind. Barking and howling of sled dogs fills the air when the wind softens to a lower shriek. There is a constant blizzard and the moonlight is weak and fitful.

John Ball leaves the vehicle beneath a drift and greets the dogs and a driver as old companions. Then he begins to mush the team of sled dogs across the snow. He seems to be a native, except that he sometimes uses a lighted compass. He keeps watch for pursuit or local opposition.

'Perhaps I should check in at the office.' John mutters.

John produces a satellite telephone and pushes a button. A voice answers,

The boss, Nigel Orr, exclaims through the ether, "Where the hell have you been?"

"On a moonlight cruise, sir."

"Well, quit fooling around. We have serious business going forward!"

John notices a glow in the blizzard.

"Yes, I'm sure. Don't be alarmed at the loud noise you may hear next."

John swerves. A rocket lands in the snow where he would have been. It waits a moment before exploding. John tosses his telephone into the snow. He mushes swiftly away from that location. The telephone explodes. The dogs pay no attention to the second explosion and neither does John.

Two days later John and the dogs part company with affection. This day is not much brighter than night in the arctic, on the Bering Sea. He sees the ship he expects and boards it, calmly assessing the faces he meets. They seem friendly, which is seldom a good sign.

When they are well at sea someone tries to stick a knife in him, so John begins to break arms, knees, and necks. The fishermen are all trained killers, but so is John. Soon there are only two contestants alive or functional on the ship,

John Ball and a Chinese agent are on a primitive fishing ship amidst ice floes. Several bodies lie crumpled on the deck. John is bent backwards over the rail, about to be knifed by the Chinese agent.

John says, in Cantonese, "I enjoyed meeting your mother in Shanghai."

The Chinese agent reacts fiercely, but John turns the tables and finishes the agent.

John remarks, "She smelled nicer."

John tosses the bodies, weapons and radios of the Chinese overboard. Large sharks come to feed. John speeds the ship toward Alaska.

A few days later John arrives at night in an Alaskan port. Now he is dressed as a local fisherman, with a stubble of beard and a faint odor of American whiskey.

There is a cruise ship docked, in addition to the fishing boats, yachts, and oil tankers.

John discards anything specifically Chinese and then he debarks from the boat with a small bag. He walks until he finds a smack with a coat draped over the wheel. He takes the coat.

"I'll be returning it soon, buddy."

John continues to a shop still open near the wharf.

Later John approaches the boarding ramp of the cruise ship and hands the purser his papers and ticket stubs. John is wearing new tourist clothes, rich tourist clothes.

John boards the ship in a suit and overcoat and fur hat. He tips the Mate and joins the crowd in a bar. A woman in her late thirties, drink in hand, sways through the crowd seductively toward John. She smiles in a familiar manner.

"John, I thought it was you! How are you, and why didn't you call?"

"Okay, okay, I was wrong, Cathy. You could have called, you know."

"I did call. You were off on another securities gambit, weren't you?"

John notices people who enter after him. One man seems suspicious.

"I'm all business. Are you with someone?"

Cathy raises one eyebrow. "Perhaps."

John smiles and leads Cathy out onto the observation deck, where he places himself to observe who might follow.

Cathy leans against a rail almost touching John and purrs.

"Not at the moment, darling; but will everything be the same?"

"Better, I hope." He gives her a light kiss on the nose.

The suspicious man comes out of the lounge. A woman also drifts out. They take flanking positions.

"I won't let you hurt me this time, John dear."

"Yeah, you probably owe me one, come to think of it."

"Owe you! Owe you one what?"

"Relax Cathy. Let's find a table and lose some money?"

They stroll inside and find a gambling table. The suspicious man and woman casually follow.

Quite a crowd is in the gambling salon of the cruise ship. John and Cathy find their way to a table.

In another part of the salon, Kiri Wan, a beautiful part-oriental woman watches John and his companion. Kiri takes note of the interest of the suspicious man. That man senses her and turns.

"Would you like to chat, handsome?"

Kiri presents herself seductively to the suspicious character.

He has the eyes of an assassin, cold and hard, neglecting to enjoy the loveliness Kiri presents. "No. I don't chat. Try someone else."

Kiri pretends to be miffed. She moves away. She uses her compact to inspect her face and take a picture of the suspect.

"Am I not pretty enough?"

The assassin turns away. Kiri sends the photograph and closes her compact.

Back at the table, John has a pile of chips. A neighbor player admires John's luck.

"Got any stock tips? You seem to win at everything."

"Well, I wouldn't buy that hot toy stock just now."

Many at the table turn to listen

"You mean Otoys? But they have got the world market cornered, and their earnings ratio is off the charts!"

John shrugs.

"Exactly. It's rather too good, don't you think?"

"I thought you said you were into risky things. Are they too much of a sure thing for you?"

"The opposite. Maybe it's just me. I'll stake this pile, that Otoys comes down to nothing by next quarter. Any takers?"

The players and spectators stare and laugh nervously, but no one takes the bet. Two people place cell-phone calls.

Much later on the observation deck John leans on the rail, looking to sea as the ship travels. He seems relaxed. Moonlight just outlines the pattern of waves.

Suddenly the Assassin strikes from behind. John is prepared. He seizes the Assassin, breaks the man's neck, looks in his face, and then throws the man overboard.

"I'm so glad it wasn't the woman."

John turns toward the salon. There the drinking and games continue but the crowd is much thinner. Kiri's face appears at the windows. She smiles at John. John returns a slight smile. He returns to the gambling salon slowly.

John locates Cathy in the crowd and approaches her.

"I'll dance with you, my lady, if you'll buy a poor man a drink."

Several people laugh at the notion that John could be poor, since he won almost all the money in the room earlier.

"There is no band. Is there a band in your room?"

"Let's go find out."

As they pass Kiri, John winks at her, suggesting silently that she could come to the dance also.

CHAPTER III

RISK MANAGEMENT SERVICES

It is a bright but overcast day on the docks of San Francisco, with tourists debarking, automobiles glittering in the parking lots, sailboats in the bay, the sounds of traffic and boat horns and children at play on their skateboards and bicycles. Vendor carts ring their bells, Trolleys groan on their tracks and a group of street musicians produce a condensed version of 'Victory at Sea' by Elgar.

When John walks from the pier, he is run into by a skateboarder. Other men run toward him and a van's tires screech as it comes around a corner. John leaps to his feet and grabs the skateboard. He wheels down the walkway.

Cathy calls out, "John! Call me!"

The pursuers chase John. Two vehicles come toward him from opposite angles. Gun barrels flash. John makes the skateboard leap and spin over one vehicle. He runs down an alley, where he finds a bicycle, which he carries up some steep steps. He ties his coat around his waist and rides toward a park. Cars roar nearby.

"Poor Cathy. Ditched again! Tsk."

John gets his bearings. He hears a push-cart vendor coming. When the push-cart is close, John walks the bicycle alongside. One of the pursuit vehicles drives past and screeches to a halt. John takes off downhill on the bicycle, going airborne several times.

Car horns blare. There are near misses. A pursuit vehicle appears at the bottom of the hill. Armed men get out and take aim. John comes too fast. One of the attackers becomes a ramp for John's bicycle. John vaults over the vehicle, careens off a dump truck and lands in a sand truck.

"Where's the ocean?" John brushes sand from his face and hands.

One of the pursuit vehicles spots John's head above the rim of the dump body. The men commence firing. John is protected by the sand, but trapped. The attack vehicle comes closer. One of the villains attempts to climb aboard, but John throws sand in the man's eyes and smashes his hand. The man falls and is run over. No one notices but John.

John rips the shabby truck bed cover into strips and ties them into a rope. The truck goes out over the Bay Bridge. The pursuers commence throwing grenades up into the dump body. Some grenades fall into the traffic. John ties the handles of the grenades down with scraps of the dump cover. A grenade in the street explodes. The traffic comes to a halt. The villains swarm out of their car and up the sides of the dump truck. John throws his canvas rope end over a projecting bolt of the superstructure of the bridge. He swings forward and away from the dump truck on his canvas rope while pulling the string on the grenades.

The grenades explode, the span collapses, the villains fall. John lands safely on the rail of the next span. He escapes on foot until he finds a friendly driver who gives him a ride.

CHAPTER IV

DUBLIN

In an exclusive club dining room in Dublin, John Ball sits alone at a plush table. Trevor Nigel Orr, head of BHC Limited (parent company of Risk Management Services), sits alone at another table. Charles Nought sits at a corner table where he can observe. There are other diners, among whom is a woman whose eyes are seen occasionally reflected in her compact mirror. It is not Kiri (It is Anais in disguise).

John and Orr are having a conversation through earpieces while pretending not to take notice of each other.

Orr mumbles, "Buster, we think that the problem in the Chinese plant is not merely an aberration. You must learn whether Laros Opecoe is encouraging that sort of thing generally. He may even be involved with some tactics which limit his competition in more dramatic ways."

"More dramatic than child slavery?" John speaks without moving his lips, but his voice is quite distinct, although almost silent.

"Indeed. Extortion, disappearances, bribery, that sort of thing. It may be just a few rotten apples, or my old friend Laros may be rather more shady than I had thought."

A tall blonde in a stunning outfit enters the room wearing a bored smile. She looks around, takes off her sunglasses, and strides toward John's table.

"I want you to meet your new minder, Buster. This is Gloria Brazed, and she will keep a rein on you. She is quite capable, as I am sure you will find. Try not to damage her too much."

Gloria sits opposite John as if she was expected, and yet as if she has little interest in being there.

"Hello, my dear Gloria. Can you pay your way, or stay home?"

She replies with a faint grimace, "Buster, you are so droll. Could you say something interesting, for a change?"

"My name is John. I despise that name, Buster. Please call me anything but that."

"As you wish, darling."

She looks away as if wishing for a rescue by a white knight. Some older men in the room are already appraising her value to their enterprise.

A waiter in a tuxedo approaches. "What is Madame's pleasure?"

John smiles slightly.

"Madame is on a diet. Do you have any dishes which are guilt-free?"

"Absolutely. Perhaps artichoke salad with balsamic vinaigrette as appetizer, then a cream of broccoli soup, and an entrée of Portobello mushroom salad brisée?"

"No." Gloria slightly rolls her eyes in distaste."

"Bring Madame the spinach salad with feta and capers, extra virgin oil and a twist of lemon, to start with."

"You are being an ass, John."

John waves the waiter away.

"I'll grow on you."

"You will be the first wart I remove by freezing."

The waiter returns with the salad. John inspects it, but Gloria won't even look at it.

"Do you mind? I'll try it myself."

John takes a bite of the salad and a sip of his wine. Then his face turns red and his eyes bug out. He rises, tosses down his fork and glass and seizes Gloria's hand.

"Poison me, will you!"

Orr looks startled. Charles pretends no interest. Another man in the room retreats. John pulls Gloria with him toward the lavatories. Gloria screams softly.

John pulls Gloria into the bleached air of well-decorated, posh lavatories.

John regurgitates into the sink. Gloria shows concern. John maintains his grip on her arm.

"It wasn't me, John, I swear!"

John drinks some antidote from a phial.

"I know. I just did not want to pay for that dreadful meal. Orr's choice, not mine."

John leads Gloria outside.

John and Gloria wait to see who might follow them out of the club. No one comes. However, suddenly John is attacked from behind.

"Hai!"

John flips the ninja and they exchange blows of feet and fists.

"Hi, yourself, laddie!"

Gloria looks for an opening. John's expressions warn her not to interfere.

"Aunh! ha! huu-ah!" The Ninja yells. Each yell accompanies a new blow to John.

John is knocked down and partly unconscious. The ninja prepares to deliver a death blow.

"Buster! Wake up!" Gloria says.

Gloria delivers a mighty kick, planting her spike heel in the rectum of the ninja.

"Aieee!" the Ninja says.

The ninja runs away as well as his pain will allow.

John regains consciousness slowly.

"You didn't have to do that, Miss Brazed."

Gloria helps him to rise.

"Then I won't do it next time. Ruined a perfectly good knock-off."

Gloria kicks her shoes into the shrubbery. She takes a pair of slippers from her clutch and puts them on her feet. John has already hailed a cab. Gloria must run to catch the ride.

CHAPTER V

AWAY WE GO

The monitors, phones, and other communications systems in this airport are marked with the logo of AndoSys Communications.

John and Gloria are at the ticket counter. Gloria faces out. She is in the cocktail dress, overdressed for travel. John is in an ordinary suit. He winks at the ticket agent.

"Rio de Janeiro, please."

"Will that be round-trip for two, sir?"

"One-way for two. We're going around the world."

"Baggage?"

"Nothing to lose this time. She's enough."

John winks slyly and elbows Gloria.

Gloria sniffles. "I won't go without some decent clothes!"

John takes the tickets from the agent. He leans casually on the counter.

"Then don't. Perhaps this lovely lady would like to come along".

Gloria goes in search of shoes and clothes in the airport shopping.

John turns his charm on the ticketing agent. "Well, Miss?"

"Fortunately, Mr. Ball, I've already been 'round the world' several times."

"Not yet with me. I would remember."

Later John and Gloria are in an airport pub. It is a decorator's version of a cozy pub, expanded to hold hundreds of people at a time.

John and another man sit at the bar. Charles Nought and another man are at tables nearby. Gloria is also at another table, stirring a drink with the staff of a miniature paper and bamboo umbrella. She rises and leaves with a discontented mien.

Gordy Jenkins says, "Mr. Ball, I know you are well situated in the securities investigation field, and that is why I am prepared to offer to double your salary if you will assist my group of investors in their due diligence and help us to make wise decisions."

"A very generous offer, Mr. Jenkins. You do know: I specialize in risky things? Your people may prefer safer investments?"

Gordy grins.

"That's the old thinking. I've set us a new course, and I think you are just the ticket! Will you drink on it?"

Gordy raises his mug.

Gloria returns with some shopping bags and wearing a business suit and flats. Many eyes are on her, for she is quite attractive.

John says, "Gordy, you're on! A toast to risky management! I'll take your offer!"

John slaps Gordy on the back, and the two men march out of the pub arm in arm, cheering for themselves. Gloria chases after them to find out what is transpiring.

"John! What are you doing? What about Rio?"

Charles Nought and some other people follow discretely behind John's parade.

"Fie on Rio! Let's celebrate, my dear. Paris! Rome! Melbourne and Sydney!"

Gordy is winded and cannot keep up. He disentangles from John.

"Call me! We have a deal!" Gordy says, with difficulty.

Gordy falls behind, returning to his gate. John continues, buying tickets at several different airlines, for various destinations, conflicting times and routes. Gloria follows, but at some point she loses him and shows her frustration.

In an airline cabin, Aer Lingus uniforms are on the stewardesses. John is in a window seat, looking out, waving to Gloria, who is behind the wall of glass of the building. At least one of the followers has made it onto this plane.

"Please buckle your seat belt, Mr. Ball. We'll be taking off, now."

John buckles up while giving a fetching smile to the stewardess.

The airliner flies above the clouds. Shades are pulled down and passengers doze off or work on laptop computers.

John and an assassin struggle in the dark among the baggage and refrigerators. At last, John prevails. He drags the body of the assassin to a floor hatch and deposits the man in the recess below the hatch. Then he straightens his clothes, ascends in the dumb-waiter and emerges into a darkened hall beside the galley.

The stewardess is startled. "Mr. Ball! May I help you?"

"As sure as the sunrise, you may."

John closes the curtain and embraces the stewardess.

A lot of time passes and John changes flights several times.

An airliner is landing in Rio, amidst beautiful panoramas of the ocean and mountains.

John meets Gloria with flowers when she arrives. She tosses the flowers in a trash can.

"Would you like to shop, dear?"

Gloria stops in front of a store window. She seems to be admiring the fashions, but she is watching the people who follow them.

"Yes, John. I would like a new Uzi, some concussion grenades, a bit of plastique, a good fish-knife, some cyanide caplets, and a few other knick-knacks. I will need them soon. Do you know a smart shop?"

She smiles at him invitingly.

"You will be glad to know your trousseau is ready for your approval, dear. Do you see that charming brick and the bodice there?"

"Yes, and I see a pair of alligator pumps I could die for, over there."

John caresses her back while putting some weaponry in her purse and hand.

"You may be useful as well as attractive, my dear." They soon exercise the skills they own and the tools they favor to demolish some of their unwanted company and they evade others.

In a clothing stall in an outdoor market they catch their breath and resume their cool demeanor. "I hope that is not my blood on your cuff, my dear."

"You wouldn't be able to see it if it were yours, John. I need to shop again."

"Oh, dear. Not again. Shall we go uptown?"

CHAPTER VI

ROAD TRIP

Many people are using telephone stations in an international airport communications area, beneath a large logo for AndoSys.

Charles Nought, agent for Orr but also for the Brown Group, reports to Orr.

Charles says softly but distinctly, "BHC, be advised that the materiel ordered has been delivered intact, despite rerouting. I am monitoring the delivery."

Charles terminates that call and initiates another.

"Objectives are in sight. Shall I conclude the transaction, or delay? There seems to be competition for the contract. Please advise."

Charles Nought suddenly realizes that he has lost sight of Ball and Brazed. He rushes toward the last place he saw them. He notices someone else displaying the same symptoms and decides to follow the competition.

Night on the streets of Rio is almost as bright as any sultry day in the pleasure dome of Brazil. Near the airport there are flashy modern cars and people. John and Gloria are being chased and driving as only professional road warriors may.

Some of the expensive autos sharing the concourse are damaged and must retire. Many horns honk in protest. John smiles and winks at Gloria.

"I admire your style."

Gloria sighs and relaxes despite the bounce and side thrust of the chase. She repairs her lipstick and takes a photo of the pursuers with her compact.

As the chase progresses, less desirable scenarios emerge, until the chase delves into the favelas and refuse heaps which surround the modern city.

John and Gloria begin the chase in a new Audi. They are pursued by a Hummer, a Mercedes, a Jetta, a Mini-Cooper, and several powerful motorcycles. Each vehicle suffers enormous damage. At last, the Audi falls into a dark, wet mess.

"We may have run out of wheels."

They are mired in a sludge heap after having been airborne and spinning, burned, exploded, crashed, caromed, rolled, quashed and shafted. Around them is a raging street battle between rival gangs and the pursuit cadres still have bullets and live killers fast closing on their position.

"At least we landed right-side-up this time, John.".

They grimly crawl out of the destroyed vehicle into the muck. Gang thugs laugh at them and converge on their position. Only the flying bullets keep the gang from terminating the touristas.

When John reaches solid ground, he perforce enters into capoara combat with dancing kickers, slashers, bashers and mashers.

Gloria is attacked separately. Both of them must run, jump, spin, flip, kick, punch, butt, and cram their way through the gnarly pathways of the favela and through the shacks and huts, wash-lines draped in rags and partial houses made from packing crates. They pause to reconnoiter. John turns a corner cautiously. He hears a moan from Gloria.

When John finds a break through which to run, he can't find Gloria. She has been captured and subdued. He leaps roof tops until he sees Gloria being dragged through a doorway by an oriental gang.

He doubles back, taunts a rival black group to follow and then leads them to the oriental compound. During the mayhem between the two gangs, Ball rescues Gloria.

Each of them has little left but underwear and tatters of clothes.

"I never have anything to wear to the dance."

John helps her to stand.

"Still bitching about clothes, are we? Don't I show you a good time?"

They steal clothes from windowsills and clotheslines, dressing in a maudlin vagabond manner.

"Too bad you ditched our ride".

They walk out of the slums into a somewhat better area. The hotels are far away.

"You can drive next time."

CHAPTER VII

SHOPPING

John and Gloria walk among patterns of flashing neon and gleaming automobiles. They hold hands like teen lovers. When they come across a street hydrant which has been opened, they dance in the spray, creating a display of colored lights festive enough for carnival.

This fashionable Rio de Janeiro store is for rich residents. John and Gloria are dressed as favela gypsies. John must demand service by imposing his most charming disdain upon the clerks. He presents a black credit card and the store manager begins to behave like a guilty puppy.

Gloria chooses several expensive dresses and accessories. She tries on one which she wears out. John selects a suit, some slacks, shirts, ties and shoes, wears some and has the rest sent to his hotel. The clerks are at last impressed with the total bill.

"Please call a limo for us from the hotel."

The clerk goes to perform the service.

"I'm keeping our last wardrobe also."

"Plan on slumming again soon?"

"I'm with you, aren't I?"

They leave the shop with clerks in tow carrying gifts from the store manager.

Gloria leans on John's shoulder in the limousine, relaxing into a romantic feeling, until a car backfire makes both of them duck. The driver laughs and John grins.

They arrive at a five-star hotel where service is gloved and obsequious. John and Gloria enter in fine clothes and are treated as royalty.

"Your suite is ready, Mr. Ball. There is a gentleman who would like to speak to you." The concierge attempts to show deference, but instead, he appears to pretend to familiarity.

A businessman in a fine suit waits nearby. He is bald and shaped like an accountant, with thick glasses.

"Very well, Louis. May we have a room for our conversation?"

Louis beckons the accountant and then leads the three to a reception room, closing the door after making sure they want no other service. John tips the concierge.

"Mr. Ball, I hope you are having a pleasant stay in Rio de Janeiro. I am Anatoly Mor. I work for Otoys. You have asked for a tour and information about our local manufacturing contractors. I have arranged to show you whatever may be of interest to you tomorrow, if that is convenient?"

John sits on the edge of a table and toys with a flower arrangement. He allows time to pass before he replies, to gage the accountant's level of anxiety. Gloria reclines on a divan, in a pose reminiscent of the gilded age.

"Yes, of course. Would you also be so kind as to provide me with your financials? I wish to be thorough."

"Certainly. I will email a set to your hotel tonight, with the password pekoe8, for your eyes only, if you please. Oh, yes, we have this example of our latest product for your amusement."

Anatoly smiles and places a plastic truck on the table.

Later in a penthouse suite of the hotel, sumptuously and sensuously appointed with flowers, candies, liqueurs and hors d'oeuvres, John Ball puts money into the Bell-boy's pocket. Gloria enters regally, appraising these appointments. The Bell-boy carries the truck toy on a platter.

"There, if you please. Thank you. That will be all."

The Bell-boy places the platter on a table. The Bell-boy backs away, turns and leaves, softly closing the leather-padded doors.

Gloria poses on a settee in her most elegant manner.

"Life-styles of the decadent?"

Ball uses a letter-opener to open the bonnet of the toy truck. A camera and battery is exposed.

"We are cover models. We are in our own reality series, it seems."

Gloria commences to undress. In dishabille, she dances over to the dimmer switch and lowers the lights.

"I can improve our ratings. Would you like to shower with me?"

John places a blanket over the truck toy. He eats an hors d'oeuvre.

"Don't make a pig of yourself. I'm going for a drink. Mind your purse, now. I wouldn't put much faith in the service here."

Gloria smiles and parades nude into the bath. She takes her purse with her.

"Don't be long, darling. I might die of boredom."

The door closes.

In the hotel bar, John takes a stool. He asks for a pint of Guinness by gesturing to the barman. He takes note of the patrons and wait-staff and unbuttons his jacket.

"Could you procure a corsage, Alonzo?"

The barman reaches into a cooler and presents an orchid corsage.

"Thank you."

John takes the corsage to a table where an exotic beauty sits. She glances up at him. John presents the corsage.

"May I join you?"

The woman makes a slight gesture of acquiescence. She is the woman who was in disguise in the exclusive Dublin club. Her name is Anais Ikk as John has discovered.

"Do you sell flowers, Mr. Ball?"

John sits across from Anais and appraises her. He gestures to the barman. John's smiling eyes seem to drink her like champagne.

"I'm all business. Please call me John. Who is it that watches me and knows my name?"

Anais fondles the corsage. Her fingers are delicate, long, and terminated with blood-red bullet-shaped nails. A waiter brings two champagne glasses and a bottle in an ice bucket. The waiter presents the bottle for inspection. John smells the cork and glances at the label and nods. The waiter pours the champagne and retreats.

Anais lifts her glass. John prepares to make a toast.

"Anais is my name. Are you working for Otoys, or against them?"

She challenges John with her eyes.

"I am investigating the company, that's all. What can you tell me?"

John touches her glass with his and lifts the drink so that he may see through the liquid for a moment.

"To clarity, then?"

"Clarity it is."

They sip. John pins the corsage on Anais' dress. She does not react to the brush of hand on her breast, but keeps her eyes nailed to John's eyes.

"You know that Laros Opecoe is part of the Brown Group? Otoys is a front for his ambitions."

John lets his eyes dip to her corsage and return to her mouth, then her eyes. He pretends to know what she is talking about, but it is new to him.

"There seem to be others with similar ambitions. Do you have ambitions, Anais?"

Anais is startled, as if she had been discovered.

"Since you are so perceptive, John, I will tell you…"

The waiter hovers near. John interrupts Anais.

"Would you kindly take this to the lady's room, with caviar, strawberries and cream?"

The waiter goes to fetch the other items. John rises and offers his hand.

"Shall we?"

CHAPTER VIII

CHALLENGES

John tips the waiter, who leaves. John turns to see that Anais holds a gun on him. He smiles.

"I take it you don't care for strawberries?"

Anais motions him to the couch. John complies.

"Don't move."

Anais gets the hair dryer from the lavatory and turns it on high. John is amused. Anais motions him to approach.

"This is odd foreplay, you know."

Anais takes his gun and steps away two steps.

"If you work for the Browns, you will not leave this room. Tell me why you are investigating Otoys."

The noise of the hair dryer disguises their conversation.

Charles and some technicians in a surveillance room can see what is happening, but cannot understand the conversation.

"Put a filter on that. Now!" Charles demands.

He makes a call.

"There are spots on the fur. The pet which flew the coop is trying to lay a clutch of new eggs. Send new farmhands and more fencing materials."

Her room is dark except for moonlight. John and Anais are entwined romantically in sheets.

"Will you join me?"

"The Yellow Group is not for me, Anais, but we share common interests. I am joined with you as far as the destruction of Laros goes."

"He is not alone. I believe that AndoSys Communications is a part of this."

"No wonder my telephone has become tricky."

"They see and hear everything." She licks his ear and shudders.

John kisses Anais.

"I hope they enjoy it as much as do I."

John gets out of bed and begins dressing. Anais does the same. They embrace again as Ball opens the door to leave. Gloria is outside waiting. She sees Anais entwined with John.

"You could have taken a cold shower with me."

John grins, releases Anais, exits the room and closes the door. He leads Gloria despite her offended, uncooperative behavior, toward the elevator.

"That still sounds enticing, my dear. There are so many pleasant new things I would like to tell you, in the shower."

They enter the elevator. Gloria pulls him close and puts a gilt fish-knife to his throat.

"I have a few choice things to tell you, darling. Like how well the plumbing works in this fleabag hotel of yours, and how I spent my time while you were playing with that siren."

The elevator door opens. Some guests enter. Gloria moves the knife down to John's groin, even as she seems to be cuddling and seducing him in front of the tourists.

The others exit. The doors close. The elevator rises to the penthouse suite, where they are staying. By that time, John has taken the knife and used it to disrobe and seduce Gloria. He forces her into the room at knifepoint. She clutches to the pieces of her designer gown.

The rooms of the penthouse suite are dimly lit with warm lights. The furniture is turned over and destroyed; a glass door to the balcony is shattered.

Gloria begins to disrobe John, pulling him toward the bathroom.

"You have redecorated, I see."

The water is running in the shower. Gloria pulls the curtain aside somewhat, revealing the body of an oriental assassin, bleeding out.

"I just couldn't wait for you to come home, John."

John uses the knife to open a few more veins so the body will bleed out more quickly. He then drapes towels over the mirrors and anything which might conceal a camera and he turns on the hair dryer.

"Life in the fish bowl, dear. They know when I am out."

"We can jam most of that."

"You did well, Gloria. I appreciate your help. Let me tell you about the Browns and the Yellows and other team colors. I hope you are not blue?"

Gloria shivers and snuggles for warmth.

"My eyes may be turning green. Anais Ikk is beautiful, but I hear she is deadly."

John gets all the robes and towels available, puts many of them on Gloria and leads her to the destroyed bedroom.

"I'll just take care of our guest."

John wraps the dead assassin in the shower curtain, scans the hall for a laundry chute, reconsiders and then takes the body to the top of the machinery on the roof, where he unwraps it and looks to the skies.

John and Gloria, well-dressed and calm, are in the lobby at the concierge desk. Gloria wears a close-fitting cerise dress. She has the attention of the clerk.

"We would like to speak to the manager, please. If you have a computer room for guest usage, please let him meet us there."

The clerk nods and leads them to a room with several computers. Gloria wastes no time finding the surveillance feed. She also finds the control room audio and puts that on speaker.

Charles' voice comes over the audio feed. "That's correct. She made intimate contact with Buster and recruited him to Yellow. No, other parties made the failed attempt on Butterfly. You must try other means. They have frustrated the normal methods..."

The hotel manager enters and John leads him closer to the monitors.

Charles' voice continues, "... I will tell RMS that she has defected and is assisting Ball against Orr. Try other means, I say."

Gloria smiles up at Gerard, the manager, who is perplexed. Gloria turns on the cameras for several different rooms, showing many guests in compromising activities. Then she shows the footage of the attack of the ninja on herself while she showered and how she defeated him.

"How do you like our little reality show, Gerard? Darling, would you set up a live feed to some hotel association in Europe, and also send clips to U-Tube?"

"Easy enough."

The manager is terrified.

"I beg you, please do not! They will kill all my family!"

"Who?"

Gloria puts the monitor on the feed from Anais' room. There are intruders entering and preparing to attack.

"John! Look! Anais!"

John gives a hard look to the hotel manager.

"Gerard, where is that control room!?"

Gerard pulls out his hair and falls to his knees.

"Basement, room thirteen, behind the boilers!"

John and Gloria rush out. Gerard watches in horror as the intruders attack Anais, live on the monitor.

John goes down the stairwell and Gloria runs up. John enters the basement room while Gloria is still running up the stairwell to assist Anais.

John enters the surveillance room politely, but holding a pipe.

"Enjoying the show, gentlemen?"

They are startled. John begins destroying the control room and eliminating the technicians. Charles Nought escapes. John finishes the disruption of the room and chases Nought. The basement halls are an obstacle course and a maze. Nought fires his gun, turns over barrels, opens steam vents, hides and ambushes John. John wants to capture Nought alive for questioning. He fires and wounds Nought. Nought escapes.

John charges toward the door to the stairs.

Gloria charges into Anais' room ready to fight, but no one is there except a dead assassin. The balcony door is open and Gloria sees a rope falling away from the rail. She moves cautiously onto the balcony, looks up and down, sees nothing and then turns.

John is behind her. She reacts strongly.

"Quite a view of Rio, isn't it?"

"Shall we go sight-seeing?"

John holds her as she begins to control her anxious agitation.

"We may be able to enjoy a bit of privacy now. I would like to find Anais, but we have no clue where to look. Unless, that is, this person can tell us."

John and Gloria inspect the corpse, but find nothing. It is obvious that this assailant was neither a ninja nor a local, but that is all they can tell.

John wraps the dead man in another shower curtain and takes him to join the other on the roof. The other body is no longer there.

Back in the room, John calls for maid service. He holds Gloria until she calms down. She kisses his neck and sighs.

CHAPTER IX

NOUGHT

"Thank goodness for maid service!"

She reclines wearily on the bed. John tours the room, looking for cameras and microphones. He finds the toy truck beneath the bed and tosses it out past the balcony.

"They weren't thorough enough, my love. By the way, I have been quite aroused by our adventures. How about you?"

Gloria pays attention to the forced manner John is using. She realizes they are still being surveilled and must expect another attack.

"I'm dying to show you, lover. Let me rip the clothes from your gorgeous body."

John smiles slightly as he circles the room, seeking the source of the electronic hum he hears. He also begins to strip for the amorous combat he has invited.

"I'm considering how many ways to amuse and tease you, darling."

Gloria opens her purse and sets it beside the bed. She unsnaps and slides off the tight, slinky dress she wears.

"I hope you brought protection, darling. You are going to need it."

Three men leap out of the darkness of the balcony and attack.

John and Gloria battle the attackers with loose sheets, lamp vases, picture frames, chairs, and other paraphernalia of the room, including food trays and bottles. The men have ropes and wear climbing harnesses.

John incapacitates one man. Gloria snares another in a tangle of bedclothes and then kicks him unconscious.

The third attacker aims a pistol at Gloria, but John kicks the gun from his hand. Gloria catches the gun and turns it on the enemy. She shoots him between the eyes.

Three more attackers arrive on the balcony and two ninjas burst in through the door of the suite. The two groups are fighting each other as much as they are attempting to kill John, so John and Gloria each down one assailant and then grab a rope and use it to trip all four combatants, much like skip-rope. They try to corral the men with the rope but when that is not productive, John and Gloria escape to the roof and the attackers follow.

John and Gloria exit to the dark night and close the steel door. John shoves a bar through the handle and hasp, but the attack will soon burst the latch. Both shiver in the cold night air.

"I don't think they were couch potatoes."

"They are our groupies. Shall we give them act two?"

The door bursts open. John downs one more assailant. Two more men come out onto the roof.

"I'm ready for the fireworks, myself."

One of the attackers trips a wire. Two explosions get three men. The four remaining attackers pause, afraid of encountering more trip-wires. They draw guns instead and begin shooting.

Gloria fires back. John reaches into a space between machinery, retrieves some miniature grenades and then tosses them to the assailants. Three more men go down. The fourth assailant is wounded by Gloria.

Chopper blades and a wind signal that more of the enemy are landing behind John and Gloria.

"They want an encore."

John and Gloria run back through the roof access door.

CHAPTER X

ACT TWO

In the hall entry to the penthouse are three choices.

The elevator doors, the smashed door to the suite and a service door are the options. John pulls Gloria back into the suite. He tosses another pair of grenades into the hall when he hears the new assailants enter. One goes off.

"Defective merchandise? I'll complain to the management."

More boots and more heavy breathing come from the hall. The second grenade goes off. John smirks.

"Iraqi specials, you see. Must you have instant gratification?"

Gloria kicks down one of the first group of assailants who struggles to rise.

"I get a kick out of delayed pleasure, also."

John grabs a rope and takes two of the climbing harnesses.

"Here, try this."

Gloria dons the harness. Another helicopter is heard landing on the roof. John ties the rope to the balcony rail, dons a climbing harness, hooks on and grabs Gloria. They leap over the balcony into the dark.

Men with weapons enter the penthouse cautiously.

Outside the hotel, John and Gloria are many floors above ground. The view of Rio is spectacular. Nearby is the iron work scaffolding of another building under construction. The wind is blowing strongly.

"You like cheap thrills?"

John rappels with Gloria clamped to his back by her arms and legs. They run out of rope and stop.

"What do you have in mind?"

They see a couple interrupted in their lovemaking in a hotel room on the other side of the glass. John gestures to the couple to join John and Gloria on the rope. Gloria leans back in an imitation of ecstasy.

"A foursome! You are quite creative, dear. Haven't we had enough of crowds for the evening?"

John swings and catches a balcony rail and they clamber over just as their rope comes falling from above. Gloria catches the cut piece. John retrieves the part still attached to his gear. Gloria playfully snares John in a loop of the rope.

"We could play bondage with that nice couple."

"Shall we ask them?"

John and Gloria open the balcony door. The couple is frozen in fear or anticipation.

"Congratulations! Here is your wedding present."

Gloria tosses the piece of rope onto the bed of the couple. While the other couple watches, John and Gloria open the closet, take two hotel robes, don them over their climbing harness and underwear and then leave the room hurriedly.

A sign in the hallway of the hotel points to a pool and gym. John escorts Gloria in that direction.

The elevator bell rings behind them. Two assailants emerge. The chase is on again. John and Gloria burst through the spa doors.

A pool party is in progress, with a band, food and drink tables and many people in skimpy pool attire, mostly topless. The balcony is crowded with amused people.

"You're overdressed again, Gloria."

"Now who's bitching about clothes?"

They try to mingle by shedding their robes and taking refreshments. They can see the assailants beyond the glass doors. John and Gloria go to the railing, where they see glass skylights below, the scaffolding across from them, and the lights of Rio.

"If you believe, make a wish. We can fly."

He makes a noose in the piece of climbing rope and snares a projecting girder thirty feet away.

"I love pixie-dust! How did you know?"

John hitches her climbing belt to his and puts the rope through his harness attachment.

"Is this still the second act?"

They climb onto the rail together. The guests turn and stare. The assailants come through the doors. John waves to the crowd, pulls Gloria into an embrace and they leap into the darkness.

In the window-lit patches and dark spaces between buildings, the party-goers enjoy a slow-motion strobe sequence of the sensuous embrace John and Gloria perform as they fall and swing between the hotel and the iron scaffolding.

John and Gloria land without mishap on a girder. He detaches them from the rope and her from him. Bullets ricochet from the girders. John and Gloria take what cover they may.

"There seems to be more drama to come. Three acts is better form."

More assailants are coming up the construction elevators and scaffolds. John and Gloria scramble upwards, dodging bullets. The assailants follow. John knocks one bad guy off the iron. Gloria smashes the fingers of another with a steel bar.

They reach a small platform but there seems to be no place to go. They throw loose pieces of materiel down onto their enemies. A sudden sound makes them turn.

A figure in a flying suit makes a landing on their platform. John grabs the flyer. Gloria pulls back the helmet-hood.

"Anais, my dear! So nice of you to drop in on us!"

"I can't let you have all the fun. Do you remember how to undress me?"

"How could I forget? This suit is much too large for you, my dear."

"Go get a room, you two."

John unzips the flying suit. Anais has extra weapons to share.

"It's just your size, John. Now, be off. I want some alone time with your playmate."

John puts the flying suit on. He takes a pistol, a knife and some tiny grenades, while Anais puts a glide wheel and brake on a truss wire at one corner of the platform. Bullets are flying all around them.

"I'm Anais. I like you, Blondie. Wanna hang?"

The two women attach to each other and to the strap of the glide wheel. They kiss and leap into the dark.

"What's with these modern chicks?"

John dives off the platform and spreads his wings. He sees the women fast gliding away. He sees the ground and the hotel fast approaching and a knot of gunmen ahead, beside dark vehicles.

Twelve gunmen shoot at the flying target coming straight at them. Two of the gunmen are shot and fall. Then three grenades explode in their midst and the yellow flying suit streaks past.

CHAPTER XI

LANDINGS

John has a hard landing, but recovers and must begin shooting immediately at more attackers. They are running toward him from the group of vehicles.

Cars swerve to miss John. He runs evasively toward an alley. Suddenly a battered Alfa Romeo screeches to a halt nearby.

"John! Get in!" Kiri commands.

John gets into the battered car and Kiri speeds away. The vehicles of the attackers are soon on their tail, chasing through the streets of Rio. Kiri pulls a control which releases an oil slick. Two of the chase vehicles skid and crash in fiery explosions. More vehicles continue the chase. Kiri releases a spike chain, which disables another chase vehicle. They are still pursued. When they come to a crossing of several streets with a lot of traffic, Kiri throws several bags from the Alfa which explode into dust clouds behind them. The sound of collisions is heard.

"I didn't know you had it in you, Kiri."

An attack vehicle pulls in front of them and weapons are aimed. Kiri evades, speeds up the ramp of a tow vehicle, goes airborne, descends by landing on a ramp of produce boxes and scoots down an alley.

"There's a lot you don't know about me, John."

Kiri screeches to a stop in front of a church.

"Are you looking for commitment?"

"You have wings. Be an angel and go do your job."

John gets out of the car and makes a gesture of blessing for Kiri. She speeds away. John looks for antagonists, ducks into the church entrance and sees the hotel nearby.

From the elevators, John enters the lounge in evening attire, having changed and showered. Gerard approaches in a state of agitation.

"Where is she?" John asks politely.

"I gave her a room to refresh in, after your unfortunate encounters. She is with another lady, I believe." Gerard rolls his eyes as a private comment.

"What number?" John smiles tolerantly.

"It is my own suite. There is no number."

Anais is seen approaching the lounge. She wears a cobalt blue designer dress with gold trim and five-inch spike heels.

"Never mind. Is your family safe?"

"I do not know. I have not been able to speak to them."

Anais moves evasively behind a pillar. Charles Nought is seen to be stalking her. He has something concealed in one hand. As he passes the entrance to the lounge, John Ball takes Nought's arm in a comradely way. Nought is startled.

"Nought, boy! I insist you have a drink with me! I think we may have mutual acquaintances!"

John pulls the distraught Nought into the darkest part of the lounge. John forces the man's hand open, to reveal a children's toy inside a plastic sleeve.

"Sit down, have a drink, Charles. Tell me why you seem to be stalking someone, with a charming toy present as a gift?"

"You are mistaken. I have been trying to protect you, on orders from Orr, Buster! Let me go and do your job!"

John inspects the toy. He discovers that it has a sprung needle which would prick the finger of an unwitting recipient.

"That I will, Nought. You seem to be doing more than your job. Here's your toy back."

John places the toy in the hand of Nought and closes the fingers on the device until he sees rage and fear on Charles' face.

"If you have an antidote, now would be a good time to use it."

37

Gloria approaches. She once more looks wonderful in a yellow silk gown with pearl seed decoration.

"May I join the company?"

John places a chair for her at the table where Nought is shivering in anxiety.

"Buster is the double agent, Gloria! See! He has just poisoned me!"

Nought falls toward Gloria, attempting to scratch her with the toy.

John seizes Nought's wrist before the poison prick can be delivered. He forces Nought to drop the toy on the table.

"Charles, you really must have that drink."

Gloria puts a caplet into a glass. John pours a little wine into the glass and pinches Charles' nose. Gloria prepares to pour wine-cyanide into the villain's open mouth, but waits for John's signal.

"It's just a local vintage, Charles. I hope you are not too much of an oenophile epicure? Oh, if you tell us a few things, I might order a better wine. What do you say?"

John pats Charles' coat and discovers a small bottle. He withdraws it for study. All this time, Nought's nose is firmly shut in the pinch of John's fingers.

"Wha-d-ya wad a-do?"

John lets go of the nose and pats Nought's head.

"Tell us just how Nought-y you have been, and with whom? By the way, is this the antidote or another poison?"

Nought tries to recover from the pinching. He is also suffering from a low-dose curare from the toy-prick, which makes him grow stiff progressively.

"What is your favorite color, Charles? Is it brown, blue, yellow, green?"

"Chartreuse!"

John stands, brushes his jacket, nods to Nought and offers his hand to Gloria.

"Keep a stiff upper lip, Nought! You might try the wine. It will be quicker that way."

John and Gloria stroll away. Nought struggles to move his hand to another pocket, to get an antidote missed by Ball.

Through his teeth, Nought says in a hiss-whisper, "It's not my last line, you nut-wit!"

CHAPTER XII

FRIENDS

This showy but Spartan room with a large window-wall is a board-room of Otoys subcontractor OyBrinquedos is filled with men and women in business suits.

Anatoly Mor and John Ball enter.

"Ladies and gentlemen, may I introduce John Ball, from Risk Management Services, who is here to look us over for a group of investors."

The crowd makes pleasant greeting sounds and claps. John bows politely, dismissing pretense with a wave of his hand.

"I just want a few details to reassure some nervous folks. You know how that can be. Sure and certain, there are no poison pills in your toy trucks, yes?"

The board crowd is a little uncertain about this phrasing. Many people do not understand his idiom and protest the figure of speech before settling down.

"What mister Ball means to say is that as we have nothing to hide, we shall have naught to worry us. Isn't that right, Mister Ball?"

"Quite right. Nought should worry you. Shall we go on the tour?"

A tour bus comes to a halt in a dust cloud.

When the cloud blows away the driver can see the road, but he is almost off the edge. He tries to back and turn, but the bus slides down a gravel slope and tires burst. The bus comes to a halt again. The passengers get off. Escort vehicles pull up and take the passengers aboard. The convoy continues on the dusty road. A crash is heard and they all stop.

John and others get out of an SUV. Ball is suspicious, but the others are merely unhappy.

As the dust clears, the primitive concrete factory is seen. There is a small parking lot where we may see the battered Alpha-Romeo if we look close.

"Well, we can walk to the factory!"

He sets off toward the building and the parking lot. Anatoly and some others follow, perforce.

"This is not how I planned your tour, Mr. Ball."

The bus and one of the SUV's explode behind them in balls of fire.

"I certainly hope not."

Two military helicopters descend near them. Much more dust swirls. John reaches for his weapon.

A commander announces over a bullhorn, "We are here to escort you! Do not be alarmed!"

The commander and a platoon of troopers appear out of the dust cloud. Charles Nought is behind them.

"We feel comforted, I'm sure."

Nought speaks through the bullhorn with a slight lisp, "There has been a Chinese attempt to disrupt this company! Fortunately, RMS has corrected the situation! Please continue with your program. We will protect you from further attempts."

John continues toward the factory. He notices not only the presence of Kiri's car, but he also notes a silver Audi and some other vehicles which do not seem to be so grimy as the regular workers' vehicles might be. The line of board members with Anatoly and John in the lead and Charles and the Commander's platoon go toward the toy factory.

The lobby of the toy factory has windows somewhat like a bunker, small and sparse and positioned as if for defense. The walls are grey concrete and the only decorations are plastic emblems of Otoys and OyBrinquedos, S.A.

Gloria enters the lobby from the office door. She wears a suit and dramatic eye makeup like the Brazilianas in the group.

Gloria speaks perfect Portuguese. "Good day, ladies and gentlemen! I am Gloria. May I escort you through the plant? We have refreshments for you in the meeting room just ahead."

The commander and Nought join in the tour, while the platoon deploy in the lobby and outside the building. Nought moves as close to Gloria and as far from John as possible. Nought makes eye contact with the Commander and indicates Ball is the center of interest.

From a balcony overlooking the factory floor the group watches the activity below. People attend to large, noisy machines. John notices that the equipment is in an idling state and the workers all seem to be pretending to work. The factory looks like it was just cleaned.

John moves closer to Gloria. Nought does also. Just as they start to descend the metal stairs to the factory floor, Nought trips Gloria and pushes John. Gloria takes a tumble, but recovers, holding on to the banister outside the stairs. She swiftly returns to the stairs.

"Commander! Ball is an assassin! He pushed her! She works for RMS!"

Gloria approaches Nought to kill him. The Commander puts his hand on John. John signals desist to Gloria.

Gloria protests in Portuguese, "Stop! It was my fault. I tripped. Mr. Ball did nothing to me. It was naught but an accident."

The commander lets go of John. Nought displays a silly grin.

"What possesses you, Charles, to behave in this manner?"

"I told you I was here to protect you. I am here to protect the interests of RMS first. You aren't even in second place, Mr. Ball."

The tour group is disturbed. Gloria rallies them with a wave and leads them onward toward the machinery. Nought and the Commander flank John Ball.

Gloria continues to explain the injection and assembly processes in English, French, Spanish and Portuguese)

"...and here we have the packing line, where the toys are put in little containers and then in cartons, ready to be shipped all over the world!"

Delivery doors are opened. Troops appear with weapons. The Commander grips John's arm firmly.

The commander says, "We have some questions to ask regarding the violence and mayhem which seems to follow your path, Mr. Ball. Please go with my men quietly."

"Of course."

John proceeds to the exit in a polite manner. He winks to Gloria as he passes her. She leads the tour group toward the same exit.

Just past the truck bay door, as John is being flanked by troopers, he engages in swift, destructive disposal of the troops and takes several weapons. Gloria does the same and they both begin running toward the parking lot. Some of the platoon heads them off, so they head for one of the helicopters. Shots are flying.

John and Gloria surprise the pilot of one of the helicopters and force him to take off. Gloria takes the copilot's seat. John forces the pilot to relinquish control and get out of the harness and seat. Gloria sets the aircraft down past the damaged bus. John expels the pilot.

"This time you are driving, dear."

The other helicopter is firing on them. Gloria rises to the occasion. The two helicopters do aerial battle. John destroys the other ship with small-arms fire, but Gloria's ship is hit, smoking and going down with little control. They land about a mile from the factory. John and Gloria escape their ship. The two helicopters produce multiple explosions and columns of smoke.

John and Gloria run through the desert.

"At least we landed right side up."

"Is that your mantra?"

Kiri skids to a stop in front of them. The Alpha Romeo is elevated like a four-wheeler. John looks bemused.

Kiri says, "Get in! They are coming!"

John and Gloria pile in and kiss Kiri. She speeds away.

"Is this a hybrid?"

"It runs on gall, like a Peugeot." Kiri defends her vehicle.

"This is quite an uplifting experience. We were thinking about a cruise. Are you coming with us, Kiri?"

Kiri pulls to a stop in the parking lot next to the silver Audi. The army vehicles are en route to the helicopter crash.

"I haven't fallen that far, Angel. Maybe later. I'll be seeing you."

John and Gloria exit Kiri's car. Kiri lowers the chassis to normal level. She waves and speeds away. John and Gloria get into the Audi. John takes the driver's seat after a silent contest between them.

"You had your turn. I hope you brought some of those refreshments. Make yourself useful, darling."

John accelerates out of the parking. When he gets to the road, the column of army vehicles are returning to chase them.

The army and eventually airplanes and police and assorted assassin groups chase John and Gloria cross-country, from desert to plains, through hills and farms and small villages to the coast, where John parks at a small restaurant beside the sea. There are boats of all kinds docked there. The pursuit has been evaded for the present.

John and Gloria steal a small launch and motor quietly out toward the harbor entrance. They can see headlights of chase vehicles converge on the docks and flashlights dancing their beams over the boats.

"Would you like a cruise vacation, dear?"

"All by ourselves, alone?"

Swift boats are coming. John opens the throttle wide but their boat is no match. Then there are explosions around them and their engine begins to fail. They leap into the water just as an RPG destroys their boat.

John and Gloria are swimming underwater for their lives, away from lights, but silhouetted against the fire of the boat, then against floodlight sweeps. They surface near a coral head to breathe.

They see shark fins reflecting in the light of the searchers. They breathe deep and dive, heading toward a rocky prominence. The lights follow their direction. Shot trails lace through the water. A shark is hit and thrashes, bleeding.

John pulls Gloria deeper to avoid the gang of sharks which converge on the blood. They bump against unknown things. John sees a faint glow ahead and they race to get there before their air runs out. The glow becomes larger and seems greenish.

John and Gloria surface breathlessly in a sea cave lit by glow-worms.

"Ahhh! Fresh air!" Then after a breath Gloria complains, "Ugh! Not fresh!"

"Come on! There must be an outlet."

They find footing and scramble up a lava tube, which is lit by moon and star-light. After a long climb, the surface becomes slippery. Gloria makes a retching sound.

"It smells like a toilet. Try not to touch your face."

They struggle, finally emerging into a refuse heap which seems to stretch out endlessly beneath the full moon.

In the lovely light of a full moon shining on a mountain of refuse, Gloria says, "Who was driving this time? What a dump!"

"Shall we go for another swim?"

"With our chums the sharks! Naturally! What fun! Is this the five-star tour?"

They slog through the refuse to the edge. It is a long way down to the water but they run as if they were not tired.

John and Gloria plunge wearily into the surf on a little rocky beach. They back-paddle and flip and splash each other and laugh until they hear the sound of a boat motor. Then they sink to their eyes and peer into the darkness. A grey, bulky boat slowly drives alongside the shore.

"Hey! Help!"

John begins swimming toward the boat. Gloria doesn't know what he is doing but she swims after him.

"Help us! Mister boatman! Help!"

The boat halts and a man looks over the side. He spits into the water. John and Gloria arrive.

"We fell overboard from our sailboat and it blew out to sea! Could you take us in to a port?"

"What you pay?" Capitano Lugo says.

"A thousand dollars, Jack!"

"You pay two thousand por each you, then I take you."

"No problem, Jack! Hurrah! Let's go!"

"Senhor, no call me Jack. Yo soy Capitano Lugo, okay?"

The crew put a rope ladder over the side. Gloria goes up first. Capitano and the crew whistle. John comes over the rail with a jealous-husband look in his eye.

"Can't you find a towel or blanket for the lady?"

Gloria takes shelter in John's arms. Capitano Lugo steers the boat away from the shore and picks up speed. A crew member brings a slicker coat for the passengers. John wraps Gloria closely and whispers in her ear.

"I used to serve on one of these boats. Do you know what it is?"

"Ancient. Ugly. And loaded with torpedoes."

The boat slows and stops at dawn in a harbor within sight of the yachts and gunboats. Capitano confronts his passengers.

"You the ones the army hunts. I think you pay much to be safe. How much you pay if I no turn you over to them?"

The sun rises, and on a gunboat an officer with binoculars gestures 'scramble and go' to his men. Helicopters and boats start toward the torpedo boat.

On the torpedo boat, John incapacitates the captain, puts his gun on the crew, accelerates the motor and turns the boat out to sea. Gloria takes a tumble and winds up being caught by the crew, who think they now have an advantage over John. Gloria kicks and punches and throws the men martial-arts style. Then she goes to the deck cannon, which she prepares like it was second-nature.

She soon has targets. A helicopter and a speeding boat both come within range. Gloria discourages the speedboat and makes the helicopter spew smoke but more craft are coming. Two more helicopters and several more boats are in view. There is also the conning mast of a submarine surfacing.

"John! Look!"

John turns and sees the sub. He turns the boat, aligns for drift and fires a torpedo. It is a wire-guided device, so he must wait. The crew members begin to revive. John motions them down. He points toward the submarine. Just then the sub explodes. The fireball rises and engulfs a helicopter. A small plane with pontoons continues toward them.

A toy-size helicopter finds them and puts its cameras on John. John shoots the little helicopter. Gloria nails the small plane. John turns the torpedo boat to run, but the engines fail. They are dead in the water.

"Maybe we need a new travel agent."

A hovercraft approaches. Gloria turns the cannon to take it down.

"Hold your fire. That may be the new travel agent. Look at the colors."

The blue and orange flag of RMS shows on the front of the hovercraft. It arrives. John and Gloria board up a ladder. They are assisted by some men without guns. The hovercraft speeds away. The men bring blankets and hot coffee.

Then Charles Nought enters, smiling. Both John and Gloria point guns at him.

"Now, don't be hasty! I told you I was here to protect you, and where would you be now without me?"

"Where are you taking us?"

"Wherever you like. There is a charming beach and village which I suggest, near here, but we have a range of a hundred miles or so. It seems we must go south because of the commotion you two have caused. They will have seen us, and they may have faster craft, so I suggest landing rather than running."

"All right, Nought. Let us off at the next beach. Thank you for the lift."

"You tried to kill me, and you tried to kill John!"

"That was an unfortunate misunderstanding. Please believe me, I am your friend!"

"Of course you are, Charles. Just let us off safely, and I might begin to believe that."

John keeps his gun pointed at Nought.

On a beach, in hot sunshine, John and Gloria watch the hovercraft depart. They turn to each other and laugh at their blanket garb. Then they walk like lovers toward the village.

"Do you think this is local attire?"

On a sleeping porch in the village, John and Gloria are getting some well-deserved rest. Assassins in black outfits sneak up on them. John stirs. The assassins pause. Gloria turns. An assassin puts a cloth over her mouth and nose. Another assassin puts a supercharged taser to John, who is shocked but manages to throw off the attacker. He uses his pistol to knock out another man and he rises to do battle. He downs one opponent and two others run away.

John revives Gloria and then takes the hood off the downed man. John feels for a pulse and sighs.

"I so wanted to practice my Cantonese."

Gloria says, in Sinhalese, "I might be able to learn a new tongue, if you teach me."

John replies in Sinhalese, "We would have to work with your French accent. You learned that at the Sorbonne?"

John picks up the dead man and walks toward the ocean. He tosses the body from a rock into the surf.

"I buried your brother at sea. Go tell him you care."

When he returns to the shack, there are four vehicles marked AndoSys and twenty men waiting in business suits. Gloria is already in one of the vehicles. She smiles and beckons John to join her. The business suits also encourage John politely, so he joins Gloria. The convoy departs the coast.

On a road in the jungle John glances behind at the vanishing coastal plain. Gloria is asleep on his shoulder. They have been travelling for hours. John wakes Gloria.

John speaks to the suit in the front seat.

"What sort of installation does AndoSys have in the jungle?"

"Oh, you will be quite amazed, Mr. Ball. You know, I am a great admirer of your work, and I think you will be quite interested in our proposal."

John puts his hand on the shoulder of the suit.

"I think we are going the wrong way."

John tosses the suit out of the vehicle, climbs into the front seat and smiles at the driver.

"Do you mind if I drive?"

He expels the driver. The other vehicles are honking and a shot is fired. John takes the wheel and heads off the path.

"Just as I suspected, they wanted to play chase."

The AndoSys men and vehicles chase after John and Gloria through the jungle. One by one, the vehicles are disabled and left behind. Many shots are fired, but the course is rough and no one is hit. At last the vehicle in which John and Gloria ride is damaged beyond functioning and comes to a stop in a muddy stream bed.

"At least,.."

"We landed right side up. Yes, I planned it that way."

John gets out of the vehicle and begins cutting some giant bamboo with his knife. Gloria weeps.

"Did I say something to upset you?"

Gloria gets out of the vehicle and slogs through the mud to the bank.

"It's what you didn't say."

John continues to shape pieces of bamboo.

"Thank you? By the way, you might want to help me build this raft, so we can get out of here."

Gloria dispiritedly begins to cut the bamboo and to peel strands for bindings.

"That's not it, but I am glad you can say that much. How are we going to float when all this place has is mud?"

"Have a little faith, dear."

A native nearby but unseen makes a bird call signal.

"Who-lodle."

"We have company." John says.

Natives appear all around them. Some have guns, some have spears. Some have blow-spears and darts. They look serious and point with their weapons.

Later that night in a native village after introductions and sharing of intentions, John is drinking with the natives and Gloria is participating in grinding a mash with the village women, who are also getting drunk on whatever they drink. One man is not a native. He has some city clothes on, but his hair has gone native.

"What's a nice missionary like you doing in perdition like this?"

"I fell in love, holy moley. Couldn't go back and pretend. Maybe someday. Still got the plane."

"If you aren't using it, I'd like to take it for a spin."

"Be my guest, John. Send me some good whiskey, and the plane is yours. I am god-awful tired of drinking this native brew."

"Would you show me the airplane?"

The missionary stands up shakily. John beckons to Gloria, who makes her excuses to the women. She goes with John and the Missionary into the darkness. The village women twitter and chirp. The moon is still quite bright, so when they come to the airstrip the plane and the runway shine with silver light.

"If you think I am going to forgive you just because of an airplane, you are right."

"Well, then, get in."

The missionary laughs at the absurd idea of flying at night in the Andean jungle, but he helps start the airplane and waves goodbye as the takeoff begins.

John and Gloria are flying over the rainforest in early morning. All is peaceful until the engine begins to sputter.

"I suppose we won't be shopping in Lima." Gloria shouts over the engine sputter. The engine becomes silent, but the prop still spins for a moment..

"There's a ranch. We can ride horses instead."

The engine totally stops. John glides the plane to a somewhat hard but safe landing. Two men in a Land Rover come to them.

John gets out of the plane and greets the men. "I am terribly sorry. We just ran out of petrol. Do you happen to have any?"

"Only diesel, no aero gas. Come have lunch with me, José. I call someone to help you. What is you name?

I am George. My lady is Stephanie. Many thanks to you, don José.

They all get in the Land Rover and ride back over the fields to the little estancia, where several of the rancher's men greet them. They are all heavily armed.

They get out of the vehicle. Don José leads them into a patio. Women in flowered skirts bring lemonade to the visitors. José beckons them to sit and enjoy.

"I go make call, yes. Enjoy".

The rancher's men stand around the perimeter of the patio like guards. Soon José returns and sits with his guests.

"Someone will be here soon. Do not worry. I am so very much glad that you have come to me."

"Why is that, don José?"

"Because there is such a big reward on your heads! It makes my heart burst with pride, that I have the honor of capture you."

Cars arrive at the estancia. Kiri and an important man surrounded by large bodyguards enter into the patio,. The important man steps forward.

Mr. Ball! You are a difficult man to meet. I am Laros Opecoe. I have been trying to catch up with you for several days to apologize for the unfortunate incident at the toy factory. I hope you and your charming companion are well and unharmed?

José steps forward and clears his throat.

"Senjor, the bounty is from the armia, I am expecting!"

"We will pay double their offer, senjor! If you are rested, Mr. Ball, our flight will be here in two minutes."

Kiri comes up to Gloria, gives her an embrace and slips a small pistol into her hand.

"Thank you, Mr. Opecoe. I am honored by your attentions."

A helicopter arrives outside the patio in the field. John and Gloria and Kiri and Laros and the bodyguards exit the patio and walk toward the large helicopter.

In the helicopter, John chats with Laros while Gloria studies the landscape passing below them. Kiri sits in a corner of the cabin and stares intently at Laros.

"Just how many factories do you have, Laros?"

"We contract with more than a thousand companies, John. I don't actually own a factory, although I do have a small research and development facility."

"Do you design the toys yourself?"

"Not anymore. I employ a small army of free-lance designers. If I am not mistaken, miss Kiri here, her father designed one of my most profitable products!" Laros laughs with pride. Kiri smiles politely.

On the helipad in Brasilia, Laros, two guards, Kiri, John and Gloria exit the helicopter. Laros leads them to a long limousine, which they enter. The guards join other guards in another vehicle, and these two vehicles follow yet another armed group in another conveyance.

The group enters the doors of a luxury hotel. Laros pauses in the lobby.

"Mr. Ball, you and your friends are welcome to anything this hotel can provide and I assure you, that is an extensive list. Spa, massage, fine dining, couturiers, tailors, flowers, medical attention, secretarial assistance, anything at all, you have only to ask. When you are ready, we can tour one of my contractor's factories here, and I welcome any questions you may ask."

"That is very generous of you, Laros. I hope you are not trying to influence my investigation with these trifles?"

"Of course I am, John. So enjoy it to the fullest, and give us a good report, but only if you are in good conscience. I expect nothing less than the truth from you. Now if you will excuse me, I will be off, and perhaps we will be able to do business tomorrow?"

"Very well. Thank you for your hospitality, Laros."

Gloria luxuriates in a marble bath tub with lots of bubbles. John is putting on black clothes like a cat-burglar. He also dons slacks and a jacket and a black tie.

"Gloria, did you notice the AndoSys logo in this hotel?"

"They are unavoidable, John."

"One can try."

"Drive safely. Try not to be too long. You know how bored I am while you are away."

John enters the bathroom and pats Gloria's wet hair. She looks up from her bubbles and sticks out her tongue.

"Try not to indulge too much in the hotel's delicacies. I would regret you losing your figure."

Gloria smiles and blows bubbles at him. John turns and walks toward the door. He takes a grape from the display. Gloria begins to rise from the bath, covered in bubbles.

A dimly-illuminated factory is being evacuated of its child workers. John Ball observes the loading of slave children in busses. Older children are being forced by men with weapons to clean floors and machines. John places electronic devices in hidden places where the cleaning crew has worked.

A guard raises his head and asks, "Que?"

John hides in a dark corner as suspicious guards pass by.

"Nada, cão!" another guard says.

When they pass, John moves on and places another device.

John enters a massage room in the hotel, looks for cameras, pulls a curtain and begins to disrobe. He covertly places a device beneath the massage table and another in a space between cabinets.

A masseuse enters. "Ah, Mister Ball. You are early!"

"Do I inconvenience you?"

"You couldn't possibly inconvenience me, Mr. Ball."

John takes her hand and sniffs the aroma, smiling.

"Please call me John. You wear orchids and cinnabar. That is quite engaging."

The masseuse pushes John playfully toward the table. She sees the multitude of little scars and runs her fingertips over his muscles. She tries to control her attraction to him. He puts one arm around her, and gently pulls her closer. She does not resist.

In the dark hotel room a figure lies sleeping in the bed with covers swirled about her form and pale moonlight describing her. John moves silently into the room. He approaches the bed, moving sidewise in a crouching pose. Swiftly he moves in another direction and pins another figure that was lying in wait. There is a flash of knife as it drops and a struggle. The two figures move violently, forcing and clasping until they crash onto the bed, across the immobile sleeper. One figure is rolled off the bed, oddly stiff in some ways, but limp. A stripe of moonlight plays across their faces as John kisses Gloria. She relaxes and accepts the embrace with passionate moaning.

Suddenly other black-robed figures enter the room and cast a net over John and Gloria. The two ensnared ones fight back, but they are hampered. John finds the knife and slashes at the net but it is made of steel wire inside of Kevlar rope and the knife does little. Gloria manages to slash one opponent. Then they are pulled off the bed in the net and dragged toward the door. The bleeding assassin uses electric shock weapons on them, trying to subdue their resistance.

Suddenly another figure enters the room and shoots the assassins with a silenced gun. John struggles, rises, and throws the net aside, prepared to battle some more.

"It's Kiri, John. Is Gloria all right?"

"I will be. Thanks again. How did you know to come?"

"Oh, I was just watching my favorite channel and thought I would join in the fun."

John inspects the bodies of the assassins. They are all Chinese. He takes their weapons and looks fruitlessly for papers.

Gloria picks up the pieces of her dummy decoy and strips the bloody sheets from the bed. She tosses the sheets to John. He wraps the sheets around the bodies and rolls them into the net with the help of the women.

"Kiri, this is the third time you have rescued us. Are you working for someone?"

"Maybe it is because I am in love with Gloria?"

"I'm flattered."

"Love is everything. I saw how much you love looking at Laros, when he mentioned your father."

"He destroyed my father and took his ideas. Otoys grew from that crime. Now you know. I think you will expose him. I want you to help me destroy him."

"The question remains, for whom do you work?"

"Can't a girl have her little mysteries? I help you; you help me, that is all you need to know. Are you going to help me destroy Laros Opecoe or not?"

John moves to face one of the hidden cameras and speaks carefully.

"I am all business, Kiri. I am here to investigate the Opecoe system. That is all. I sincerely empathize with the terrible history you have related but I caution that vengeance is a double-edged sword."

"Kiri, if you really love me, let's go away from all this and live in passion and joy." Gloria pleads.

Kiri is totally distraught, angry, and determined.

"Then you will both die! How could you be so cold! Are you Yellow? I saw what you saw at the factory!"

Kiri attacks John and Gloria but they subdue her and then they begin to seduce her. Gloria turns down the lights. John whispers in Kiri's ear.

"Did you forget we are on camera? I will destroy Laros, but there is more at stake than one man's fate or your desire for revenge. This man has built an empire on child slave labor, extortion, bribery, and lies. Let me do my work and I will satisfy your thirst."

Gloria strokes and kisses Kiri also. Kiri relaxes and the three become entwined in pleasure.

The room is dark but the light has changed to pre-dawn with stars visible out the window-wall. There are fluttering aerial shapes around the bundled assassins and at the foot and head of the bed where John, Kiri, and Gloria sleep.

John restlessly brushes whatever tickles him about his ears. Suddenly he awakes and sits up. The fluttering shapes whirl and flit about the room.

John turns a lamp on and sees to his dismay, that the women are covered with little bleeding wounds and when he feels of his ears, he feels blood. Gloria and Kiri open their eyes, see the blood and scream.

"Get in the shower! Use all the soap! Hurry!"

Kiri and Gloria run to the bathroom. John opens the glass door and uses anything he can to shoo the vampire bats from the room. Then he closes the glass. He opens the room door and peeks into the hall. He exits the room and returns with a bottle of bleach. He runs to the shower and begins sponging the bat wounds with bleach-soaked towels. Gloria and Kiri force him into the shower and soap him and use the bleach on him also.

"Laros!" Kiri exclaims.

Kiri kisses Gloria, leaves the bathroom, dresses and runs out of the hotel room determined to find and kill Opecoe. John is still covered in lather, and then Gloria is using the bleach on him, so he does not see Kiri leave but he senses she is gone.

"Kiri!"

"She is gone, John. Think what we must do. Those were vampire bats. We will get sick. In a few hours, we could be dead."

"No! No!"

CHAPTER XIII

FRIENDLESS

Among small planes parked on an airport apron, John and Gloria are boarding a rental plane, with several bags. They are well-dressed for adventure in the forest this time.

"Whose turn is it to drive, my dear?"

Gloria takes the copilot seat. John takes pilot and begins to start the plane.

"I don't care. The shots make me feel sick. I am worried about Kiri. Shouldn't we stay to confront Opecoe, instead of chasing after whatever evil AndoSys has cooked up?"

"I believe they are connected. I need to know how and why."

John takes off. Below, several limousines drive onto the airport tarmac.

"I will need an airsickness bag if you do anything but fly straight and level".

"Then get a bag. We will have another game of chase if my vampire vision is working."

"Maybe we should just bite them, and let them die of rabies."

Two other small airplanes take off from the little airport. John heads for the mountains. Gloria reaches behind the seat and opens a bag full of weapons.

John says, "Here they come."

John's plane is chased in aerial combat over the Andes by two similar bush planes. They shoot with machine guns and small arms. Gloria fires a small missile and one chase plane goes down. John does aerobatic maneuvers. The remaining chase plane stalls and falls. They are already at the glacier-capped cordillera and their engine is having trouble with the altitude. A sudden ice squall forces them down on the glacier.

John and Gloria pull their bags from the plane and dig for coats and weapons. They have boots but no skis. Helicopters approach. An RPG strikes the plane, which explodes. John and Gloria hide in a crevasse. Men land from the helicopters and come their way.

"Let's toboggan!"

Gloria wraps her legs around John from behind. They put one of the bags underneath them for a cushion and they go sliding down the channel of the crevasse. They soon get out of range of the grenades, missiles, and gunfire of the pursuit but they have no idea where they are going, their speed is increasing and the ride is not smooth.

"You couldn't have picked a softer slide, could you?"

"At least we are still right-side up!"

Just then they are flipped and become airborne, fall many feet tumbling and land face down in melting mush at the foot of the glacier. Gloria lands on top, relatively dry, but John is buried face-down in the mush. He slowly removes himself from the problem.

"You drive well, but your landings need work."

John and Gloria get off the high barren slopes and into the trees at the edge of the forest just as a helicopter passes overhead.

John and Gloria struggle down tangled, slippery jungle slopes. Gloria slips into a fern-covered gully. John leaps in after her and both go sliding down a torrent with muddy sides. At last they land in a clear stream, surrounded by nearly impenetrable plant growth.

"Path of least resistance?"

Just then, a movement in the water catches their attention. It is a very large snake, coming in their direction.

"Maybe not." Gloria sighs.

John and Gloria scramble out of the water. The snake passes them, but then they see in the water a school of fish which they both recognize.

"Piranhas!" they warn each other.

John and Gloria arrive at the bottom edge of the forest after much more trekking. A planted field, a small village and the rising gibbous moon seem peaceful and romantic.

John and Gloria emerge cautiously into an open field, see the view and embrace. They pause to enjoy the scene. Dogs begin to bark.

"Just what a girl wants. John, you romantic, you!"

There is a truck parked beside a cantina a dozen yards away with music blaring from a speaker. John and Gloria stroll to the building as if they are tourists but they look carefully for traps and enemies.

"How about cocktails and dinner, my dear?"

A few men in the cantina are drinking and playing a bar game with coins, to see which can edge-flip a coin over a tumbler and into a saucer. They stop and stare when John and Gloria enter. The owner approaches the table.

John asks in a local dialect of the pampas for a local barbecue dish, collard greens, sugar-cane liqueur, and corn bread with fennel.

"Could we please have caipirinha, churrasco, couve, requijao, and some broa?"

The owner nods and goes to get the items. The bar game resumes, but one of the players comes to the table.

"Welcome to our little village. I am Ernesto. If I may ask, how did you get here?"

"We flew. Our airplane crashed and we walked down the mountain. Would you like to share our meal, Ernesto? I am called Joao."

Now it is the next day. John and Gloria are riding with Ernesto in his truck toward the coast after drinking all night. Gloria is fast asleep on John's shoulder. They come to a road check with army officers. Ernesto pulls to a stop.

The officer looks inside. The odor of liquor is strong and he withdraws his head.

"Who are you?"

"I am Ernesto and this is Joao and his wife, Josefina, and we come from Gorda Mari and we will get fish for a party and if you want some of my requijao I have a bottle just for you, senjor."

The officer smiles and accepts the bottle proffered. He then waves them onward.

Ernesto and Joao sing unintelligibly as they drive away.

"Oya-vemejas-amato-eee...."

In a coastal village clothes shop Gloria admires her new outfit in a three-way mirror while John pays for their new garb. The clerk flirts with John.

Outside not far from the clothes shop John opens the trunk of the silver Audi. Gloria looks inside and smiles.

"Not all the world is populated by thieves."

Gloria closes the trunk. John searches for keys hidden in a box inside the wheel well. Then with the keys, he attempts to start the car with no success. Gloria opens the bonnet and laughs.

John goes to look at the empty engine compartment and tosses the keys up in the air. Gloria catches them.

"We still must get our things from the boot, you impetuous boy."

"Yes, mother."

They take two suspiciously heavy bags from the trunk of the car and also some softer, lighter bags.

They walk along the waterfront like carefree lovers on vacation, with no cares to trouble their young hearts.

John and Gloria enter a restaurant. They have changed into yachting clothes and applied tan makeup. They go to the bar and take stools. Gloria goes to the restroom. Two yachters are at the bar. The barman approaches.

"I'll be after having a pint of Guinness, if it may be you have it?"

The barman draws a pint and places it on the counter.

"So you are an Irishman, mate!" A red-faced, red-haired yachter says.

"Yes, junior, but I have been to Australia, and I know a dingo from a wombat."

Another yachter asks, "The question is, are you merely acquainted, or do you eat them?"

"Oh, I can make a fine stew, you may be sure of that!"

Gloria re-enters. She joins John at the bar but looks invitingly at the Yachters.

"When are we going back to sea! I am so tired of this dust and squalor!"

The yachters' tongues almost hang out with desire. John shrugs.

"Well, we can sell off the Audi and buy a boat, for sure, but it might be a wee little craft and not go far out to sea." Corky and Wayne introduce themselves and make eyes at Gloria. Corky loves cars. John talks about life as a chef on boats and the many dishes he has learned to cook from his travels. Wayne loves food. They progress outside after eating and drinking a few pints more than most people would find reasonable.

Corky is admiring the Audi. John and Gloria are coming aboard the motor yacht with their bags. The yacht is sumptuous and spacious. A sailor offers to take the bags below.

Wayne says, "Welcome aboard! We haven't had a proper cook since our Lanny fell in love and jumped ship. Order whatever you need and we'll go to sea as soon as it is loaded."

"It is sure a pleasure to be aboard, Captain Wayne." To the sailor he says, "Just take the lady's baggage and show me the way, sir. My name is John. How are you called, laddie?"

"Mbo. You new Cook?"

John and Mbo trundle down the stairs, chatting as if they are old friends. Gloria takes a pose on the deck lounge as if she is a passenger or owner rather than the cook's helper. Wayne offers her a drink and sits close to enjoy her beauty.

Wayne's female companion comes on deck and senses danger.

"Dorothy, allow me to introduce Gloria. She is the cook's friend and helper. Oh, yes, we have a new cook. His name is John, and he's as Irish as a potato."

Dorothy sits between Gloria and Wayne.

"I'm glad to meet you, Gloria. You look more like a model than a cook's helper."

John bounds up from below, grinning like a child with a new toy.

"Glory, you have to see this galley! It's a wonder! Come on now; don't be bothering the Captain and his missus!"

John pulls Gloria down the stairs.

"What an odd couple!" Dorothy says.

"What do you expect from a potato-head? I'll be pleased if he will give us a few good meals."

"Oh, I know what you want to taste!"

Night and moonlight are on the water. John and Gloria are in the launch boat of the yacht, returning to the yacht with supplies.

"They tracked the car."

"I know. I saw Nought poking around. Maybe Corky's tale floated."

"We can't just wander off to sea."

"No slow boat to China?"

"Whither thou goest, darling."

They pull up to the yacht and tie on. Mbo and another crewman come to help load on the supplies.

"Captain, he say we go Cape Town. Maybe you like Cape Town, Johney?" Mbo says softly.

"Been there, I have. A bit of a mess. Why go there?"

"This."

Mbo places something in John's hand, while they are passing a bag of potatoes. Mbo takes the sack down below. John discretely puts the little rock in a pocket. He presumes it is a rough diamond.

"Did he say, 'Cape Town?'"

"Yes. But something tells me we might not get there without a detour."

CHAPTER XIV

ON THE OCEAN

Dinner on the deck. Wayne and Dorothy and John and Gloria are being waited upon by two of the crew. Mbo is at the wheel.

"You certainly live up to your claim, John. This is the best food we've had." Wayne says.

"And the best conversations, too! I think you two are more than you pretend." Dorothy winks.

"Just a chiel with a taste for adventure, that's me. Glory is the one with a head for business."

"What kind of business, my dear?"

"She likes the pretty stones, now." John winks back at Dorothy.

Gloria looks daggers at John.

"What kind of pretty stones, if I may ask?"

"John is playing games. Don't listen to him."

"The kind of pretty stone you pay no duty on! Ha, ha!"

Gloria slaps John soundly. He just laughs. She leaves them and goes to watch the sea at the rail.

"Indeed! We may have something in common, then."

"John, come here this minute!"

John gestures to Wayne and Dorothy that he is being dragged away by a superior force. Then he goes to Gloria. Gloria points to the horizon.

"Boss! Captain!" Mbo calls.

A speedboat is coming their way. Behind the speedboat is a large freighter.

"How fast can you go, Mbo?"

"Not fast enough, Boss!"

Dorothy and Wayne rush to the rail. The speedboat is closing on them.

"We're six hundred miles from the coast! Come on, Johnny, I've got a few weapons down below. Maybe we can make them go away."

John and Wayne rush below. The women watch the boat approach. Mbo pushes the yacht as hard as it will go. Dorothy is terrified. Gloria tries to calm Dorothy. Suddenly the motors of the yacht quit. Two crew members escort John and Wayne back up onto the deck. The crew members have guns.

"Betrayed by our own crew!"

The pirate boat pulls up and the Nigerian Pirates board. They send some pirates down below, with the mutineer crew, and when they come up, they are grinning and displaying bags of small size, but apparently large in value.

The Pirate Chief says, "Nice you bring diamonds to us. Thank you. Nice boat. Thank you again."

"Okay. You got the diamonds. Now, let us go on our way."

The pirate laughs.

"Yah, you funny man. Maybe you like little boat in big ocean? No water, no food, just ocean. Learn to fish?"

The pirate chief looks at the women and smiles.

Dorothy faints. Gloria catches her.

"Better maybe you come with. Maybe good ransom. Maybe you live long, get another ship, come again, give me more! I keep woman, make baby! Now we go!"

The pirate chief motions for his followers to do their thing. Mbo, Wayne, Dorothy, John, and Gloria are handcuffed and made to sit on the deck. The yacht and the speedboat begin moving fast under the command of the pirates.

At night on the African coast, the captives are herded off the launch and into a prison compound, where there are quite a few other European and Indian captives, along with an assortment of black crewmen who are also captives. The handcuffs are removed and the pirates leave the compound, laughing at the prisoners.

"Some cruise! Next time I choose the travel agent!"

John counts the number of people in the compound.

"Will forty-two people fit on Wayne's yacht?"

"No, and it is too slow. What do you have in mind?"

"I'm not Gilligan. I did manage to bring a few trinkets, however."

John slips a knife and grenade and some diamonds to Gloria. He walks casually among the prisoners, getting acquainted. Gloria comforts Dorothy and two other women she finds.

Gloria catches guards' attention at the prison compound gate. Two pirates approach warily.

"Please, please let me out of here! I will do anything to get out!"

"You do anything we say, and no get out!"

The guards laugh and make obscene gestures.

"It's more better if you nice-nice."

"Shut you mouth, woman."

"Nya, nya-naya-na-nya!"

Gloria sticks out her tongue at the guard and makes an obscene gesture of a local origin back at him. The two guards are infuriated and unlock the gate to get at the disrespectful woman who mocks their manhood.

As soon as the guards come in, they are downed by John and Mbo. Their throats are slit and their weapons are taken. The prisoners begin sneaking out of the compound. A few must be carried.

"Now for the good stuff." John says.

John, Gloria, Mbo, and Wayne sneak aboard the swift boat. They silently kill and dispose of the crew. Then some of the prisoners are led aboard but they remain still and quiet.

Wayne, John, another ex-prisoner and Gloria board the yacht and silently dispose of the pirates. More of the prisoners come aboard and hide. John retrieves some grenades from hiding and sets out in the launch.

John returns, ties on to the yacht and comes aboard. He is welcomed by Gloria with a kiss. He uses a transmitter-trigger to begin a series of explosions on shore and at the other pirate boats.

The rescues cheer. "Hah-hoo! Hooray! That'll teach you, buggers!"

The swift boat and the yacht both start moving speedily away from the pirate city, which is on fire. Shots come their way but do no damage.

"If I were a woman, Johnny boy, I would have your baby!" Wayne exclaims.

Several people come up to thank John and Gloria. Dorothy is especially grateful.

"I knew there was more to you than just a cook!"

"Sometimes I would prefer to be just a cook. It is a high calling, to make people belch with pleasure rather than to bawl with pain. Anyway, we could not have escaped without the charms and talents of Glory."

Wayne and Dorothy and several others swarm over Glory to thank her. John grins at her discomfiture. It is hours before she can get away from her admirers.

There is a faint haze of South American land and a cloud shadow to show people on the yacht and swift boat that they are near safety at last.

Ragged and tired people rise and cheer. The people on the swift boat cheer and the people on the yacht respond.

John looks through binoculars.

"We have company. I see a destroyer and two cutters."

"I hope they like tourists. Where are we, anyway?"

"We are off the coast of Argentina." Wayne says. "There was some weather to the north."

The ships are closer now. An airplane flies overhead and returns toward the ships. The yacht's radio begins to squawk and a voice speaks in Spanish..

"Stop your engines and prepare to be boarded! If you do not comply, we will use force. Your ships are now the property of Argentina!"

Gloria takes the radio microphone.

(In Spanish) "We are escapees from pirates! Do not use force! We are civilians from many countries who have escaped from pirates!"

An explosion astern is the only response to Gloria's message.

"I won't give my boat to Argentina! What do you say, Johnny? We have a full tank, thanks to the Pirates."

Another shell hit closer to the swift boat. Mbo could be seen, signaling.

"They will think the crewmen on the swift boat are pirates, no matter what we say."

John makes a signal to 'scramble and go' to Mbo. Wayne puts the yacht into high speed and the chase begins. Several passengers wail and beat the deck with frustration. Two of them come to confront Wayne and John.

George pleads, "What are you doing? They were going to rescue us! We need food and water!"

Just then a shell explodes close enough to dash the unhappy George with sea water.

John says, "That's why. They think we are pirates, pretending to be innocent. If you trust them, go in the small boat, and see how they welcome you."

George looks worried, sees more explosions behind them and slinks away with a miserable look on his face.

"He's right about the food and water, you know." Mabel comments.

In the lowering day of the Straits of Magellan there is a lot of ice and wind. But relatively calm seas surround the two ships as they plow ahead.

"Have you sailed here before, Wayne?" John asks.

"No, but I have charts. I dreamed of doing this for years."

"I'll just look at those charts. I made it through once before, but then I couldn't see anything. This is terrific weather."

Wayne brings the charts. Dorothy takes hot coffee in cups to the bridge. She is wrapped in blankets.

"This is the last of the coffee. Where are we?"

John says, "The straits of Magellan. The end of the world. Maybe the swift boat has coffee."

John goes onto the slippery deck and waves a flag at the swift boat. Someone waves a response. A voice comes over the ice from a bull-horn.

"Are you okay?" It is Mbo's strong voice.

John picks up the yacht's bullhorn to respond.

"Food low, Coffee gone, need water."

"All same here. People sick. Stop or go?"

"Follow us. We go while weather is good. Okay?"

"Okay. We follow. Go now. Bye-em-bye, maybe bad sea."

The yacht forges ahead through the treacherous passage with the swift boat following in its wake. They have luck and make it through, but the weather is rising.

A break in a squall off the coast of Chile reveals a full moon high above, and a line of lights on shore to the right side of the ships. John wakes Gloria, who is buried asleep in his arms. He gives her a kiss and directs her attention to the lights. She smiles and turns so she can enjoy the scene.

"More beautiful than diamonds, isn't it, Dorothy?"

In a harbor in southern Chile, near Puerto Cárdenas, the rescued people are saying farewell and thank you to Mbo and Wayne and John and Gloria. Local uniformed men are processing the people. None of them have papers.

John is covertly giving each person a few diamonds. Wayne at last notices what John is doing.

"Are those my diamonds?"

"Maybe. I found them on the beach. Do you want them all for yourself?"

Wayne considers; then he waves them away with a grin. Dorothy gives a thank-you look to John and then a big warm hug to Wayne.

"I think we will look for pearls this time."

Mbo approaches the yacht.

"Now I am captain if they let me keep this boat. Mebbe I am big trader, now. Johnno, you want be cook belong me?"

John embraces Mbo, and they laugh.

"Maybe so, bye-em-bye. Good man, Mbo, good man."

Military-uniformed men approach John and Gloria.

"You are John Ball and you are Gloria Brazed!"

"If you say so, officer. What can we do for you?"

"Make it easy on yourselves and come with me quietly. Some very important people want to talk to you."

"I'm sure. Couldn't we have a light lunch and a cup of coffee first? We have been at sea without rations for a week, and it is beginning to wear on us."

The officer ignores the request. He turns and marches. The guards with him make it plain that John and Gloria must follow.

"I was so hoping for a quiet beach vacation and some good food."

They see two vehicles in the village which seem to be from elsewhere. One of the vehicles has the AndoSys logo on the door. The other vehicle perhaps belongs to the officer.

"I know a good restaurant in Chiloé."

The guards and the officer are taken by surprise and go down. John takes a weapon and shoots the AndoSys engine and radiator. Gloria takes the other weapons and gets into the officer's vehicle.

"My turn!"

John gets in the passenger side.

"Just make sure we land right-side up, this time!"

They speed away in a cloud of dust.

"You were driving last time!"

Far from the coast and the officers, an abandoned farmer's house is noxious with insects in the roof thatch and dusty, termite-infested boards but it is cover from aerial surveillance. The vehicle outside is covered with fronds and parked beneath a large mango tree.

John and Gloria are sharing a delicious and slimy mango speared on the point of a knife. They are as interested in the fun of eating as in the food.

In the night Chinese assassins sneak toward the sleeping couple in the hut.

John whispers, "Wake up, dear. We have visitors."

Suddenly snares are tripped by the assassins. They are strung up in wire nooses, gurgling their last breaths. John pulls the feet of each man in turn while Gloria relieves them of weapons. She finds a flashlight and celebrates by flicking it on and off.

"No!"

All is quiet for a moment. They begin to relax. John grins. But then they hear boots on gravel and they know there are more assailants. They remove fronds from the military vehicle and get in. They start by rolling down a steep track. John engages the motor. Shots are heard. One shell ricochets from their vehicle. They pass under a large tree. Someone drops into the rear seat. Gloria turns to shoot.

"Gloria! It's Kiri! Don't shoot the one who loves you!"

Instead of fighting they embrace. But then they draw aim on outside forces because they are stopped by a vehicle in the road and surrounded by men with guns. They leap from their vehicle and run, shooting behind them. In the darkness they are disoriented. All is suddenly quiet so they stand still, listening for pursuit. Kiri sees a figure in the darkness. She shoots, but she is shot and falls. John and Gloria shoot the assailant. Gloria takes Kiri in her arms and knows she is badly hurt. John kneels beside them, still on guard for more attackers.

"How badly are you hurt, Kiri?" John asks quietly.

"I won't be able to finish my mission, John. Promise you will…"

Kiri dies in mid-sentence.

"I will, Kiri, I will."

Gloria is weeping. John listens.

Charles Nought's voice comes over a bull-horn.

"John and Gloria! We came to rescue you! Why did you fire on us? Come on out so we can get away before the real bad guys come!"

Gloria and John both come to defensive attention.

Laros Opecoe speaks over another bullhorn.

"Mister Nought, I believe I recognize your voice. This is Laros Opecoe. I also have come to rescue Mr. Ball and Miss Brazed. We see your men. Please lay down your arms, so we may all go to a good meal and a comfortable bed tonight!"

A black-clad figure drops from a tree in front of John

"Aiee!!!"

The assassin throws something. John ducks and shoots the assassin. The man falls at John's feet.

John shouts, "Hold fire! It was only another Chinese assassin!"

Many flashlights blind John and Gloria and show the dead assassin and the body of Kiri. Gloria closes Kiri's eyes and kisses her lips.

CHAPTER XV

FLOWERS

This is Peru, a very small town. A strange assortment of people are in a small, cheap hotel chosen for being close at hand. There are masses of flowers in vases in several places in the room.

Laros is seated in a chair. Charles Nought stands uncomfortable near a dresser, avoiding the flowers. John and Gloria sit on the bed. A servant girl enters the room with a cart piled high with food and drink. She is tall for Peru.

Laros says, "As you have had quite an ordeal since last we spoke, Mr. Ball, I wish to let you recuperate before we resume our business. I hope we are still engaged and going forward? The investors are quite anxious to see your report. Please rest and we will be able to conduct business in a civilized manner tomorrow. It so happens that one of the factories which produces my toys is quite near here. Isn't that a stroke of good luck? Guards will be outside to protect you from further harm. You have nothing to fear. Come, Nought, leave them in peace for a change."

Laros rises to depart. Nought reluctantly follows, giving a last word as he closes the door.

"I will report that you have resurfaced to Nigel. I mean, to Orr."

He shuts the door.

"And elsewhere, I am sure." John says.

The servant girl takes off her wig. It is Anais.

"He is working for the Brown Group, I am certain. I tracked him to Cairo and got some of his reporting on a disc."

Gloria looks startled for a moment.

"Anais, I thought that was you! We have missed you. Poor Kiri is dead, and I feared that you might be also."

Anais sits beside John on the bed. She offers to feed him a delicacy. Gloria looks miffed.

"Is there a computer with an internet connection around here?"

"There is nothing here except a few community telephones, but even those are part of the AndoSys system. I can get you shortwave, but it would be an open channel, and the mountains interfere with the transmission."

John refuses being fed. He feeds himself a morsel. Gloria looks at the food and begins eating as if there would never be another meal. Anais takes the moment to kiss John and caress him.

"I am famished. Could we just eat?"

Anais looks as if she wants to eat John, but she reclines instead on the bed.

Just then a train whistle sounds and iron wheels brake noisily to a stop. Heavy vehicles are being off-loaded and a military radio is heard.

"We may have brought the modern world to this village. What a shame." John remarks.

Anais produces a small radio, puts an ear bud in her ear, tunes the radio and listens.

"It is coded speech. It has to be connected to AndoSys. I can't tell what they are saying."

She hands the radio and the ear bud to Gloria. Gloria concentrates, trying to understand. Anais produces a larger electronic device, tunes it to the radio frequency and pauses.

"Better not listen to this, Gloria."

Gloria removes the ear bud. Anais turns her jammer on.

Outside voices shout. "Aiee! Caramba! Oioioioi! Then they curse in Spanish.

The train is heard building up steam and beginning to move.

"Shall we?" John asks. He reaches hands to the ladies. They rise reluctantly.

Gloria groans and gathers some things. John selects a few choice morsels from the food, wrapping them in towels and pocketing them. He sips the local brew and makes a face. All three go out the window, down a roof.

They help each other get down from the hotel roof and they cross the streets to the train siding, where the little train is moving already. They meet no opposition and get on at the end of a passenger car on its rear stage. Behind them the hotel room explodes in a fireball.

"I wonder if they have a sleeper available." John asks. He leads them into the car. They find and occupy an empty compartment.

Gloria awakens because the train halts at yet another village. Dawn is near. She sees that Anais is coiled around John on the opposite bench. She makes a face and rises just as the train begins to move again. She pulls the curtain of the compartment slightly to one side, about to go out for a stretch, but she closes it immediately and puts herself on guard.

"Hsst!"

John and Anais wake up.

"Nought is on board!"

Anais disentangles herself from John. She produces a small folk toy carving and smiles.

"I can take care of that."

"Later. He will lead us to his contacts. He may not be the only mole. Do you still have your radio?"

Anais produces her radio. John tunes it. He listens for a while. Gloria continues to keep watch for Nought. Anais watches the landscape go by.

"Orr told Nought he is sending someone to meet me when I arrive. I presume he means Santiago."

John and Gloria exit the train car in Santiago and are met by a business-suited man who hands a briefcase to John and a purse to Gloria, then leaves. The noise of the train obscures the words they say. Charles approaches and leads the other agent away as if they had a previous meeting arranged.

John and Gloria stroll away from the station toward a hotel. Vendors try to sell local products to them as they walk.

"Do you think that strange?"

The telephone inside the briefcase rings. John opens the briefcase slightly and takes the phone.

"This is Trevor Nigel Orr. Buster, are you there?"

"You found me.".

"Remind me to reprimand you on that subject, your penchant for unreachability. You must go meet Laros Opecoe in Goa. He has complained that you have avoided serious discussion with him on several occasions with no explanation. This may be your last chance. You leave tonight."

"Thank you, sir, for your indulgence of my frailties."

"Are you being cheeky with me? Be warned, my indulgent nature is not to be trifled with. I'll send a replacement if you are not careful."

Anais appears in front of John and Gloria, flushed and breathless.

"Nought just killed Grainger! He pushed him off the platform in front of a truck, and then he blamed me! I am going to get him!"

"Who is that? What did she say?"

John closes the phone.

"Why were you there? I asked you to wait!"

"He is too dangerous to you and me to let him live."

"We agree on that." Gloria says.

"I'll be seeing you."

Anais disappears behind some vendor booths just as a police car passes by.

Above the clouds an airliner flies to Goa. This time no assassins have come aboard. No Chinese assassins, that is. John and Gloria sleep and dream of food.

CHAPTER XVI

DHARMA

John sits at the bar of the airport lounge in Goa to order, but the bartender points him to look at a table in a corner of the room. John finds Orr at the table.

"What a pleasant surprise, Nigel."

"I believe you have become unreliable, Buster. I am assigning Charles Nought to continue the investigation of Opecoe and Otoys. You are going to Dublin, where you will be debriefed. Gloria will go to Italy."

"You are setting a poodle to guard the wolf, Orr. Nought is a double agent."

"Precisely what Charles said about you, Buster."

"Whom do you believe, then, sir?"

"That's to be decided. Meanwhile, you are denied access to resources, and I expect you to be in Dublin tomorrow for debriefing. That is all."

"Very well, Orr, I hereby tender my resignation. Good luck with your new chum."

John withdraws. Orr fumes. Charles Nought grins from his concealment. Gloria (who is watching from a computer monitor) has a determined expression which does not bode well for anyone who would cross her path.

A stewardess with the Otoys logo helps seat Trevor Nigel Orr on Opecoe's private jet for a luxurious ride back to Dublin. A steward brings a drink.

Orr behaves as if this is all normal. He produces a telephone and makes a call.

"Did Ball get on the flight to Dublin?"

(pause)

"Then you may proceed with plan EB."

Orr closes the phone, takes his drink in hand and allows himself to appreciate the beauty of the steward.

CHAPTER XVII

ASSASSINS

Night is hot and heavy in the warrens and on the streets of Goa.

Unknown enemies chase Ball. The chase is a chain of explosions, bullets, footraces, car pileups and even a rickshaw turnover. The chase continues out of Goa toward Mumbai.

Ball blows up a plant in Mumbai, is chased again.

Military and police officials attempt to catch Ball in a roadblock, but he escapes, and is chased.

A train is derailed near a factory. Ball is seen running through slum streets.

John Ball in disguise prevents Otoys agents from abducting child prostitutes.

Beggars are lined up endlessly. One of them is John Ball.

Gloria and Anais drive slowly, looking at each beggar. Gloria recognizes John and beckons to him.

"Get in, beggar!"

John pretends not to know she speaks to him. Many other beggars converge on the automobile. Gloria and Anais escape. When they slow down and are trapped in a jam, John comes to the auto and enters as if he had been waiting for a ride.

"Stinker!" Gloria complains.

Anais looks at him with disgust.

"I am glad to see you, too!"

Both women climb over their seats to kiss him, despite his awful appearance.

"We are making a scene. Could we get a room, ladies?"

Gloria serves coffee and scones to John in a hotel room. John has showered and shaved. Anais brings a coat and tie to the table. John smiles thanks.

"Well, what have you been up to? I gather that neither yellow, nor blue and orange, are our team colors now?"

"I skipped out on the company and Orr put out the word to terminate me as well as you. I have been looking for you, following your explosions, for weeks!" Gloria says.

"Nought has been trying to catch me but he has failed so far. Yellow must wait until he falls. He must die for me to be free, and anyway I want to finish this." Anais adds.

"I need proof, documentary proof, that Laros and Otoys and Nought and the Brown group and possibly AndoSys, are all tied together in this plot. I am afraid that Orr is under their control. I found some of the toy shipments concealed bio-weapons. Many of my informants have been killed. I am down to few resources, and only two friends.

"Now I have put you in more danger."

Anais and Gloria reassure John that they don't mind the danger by their loving attentions.

John has to stop this love-fest by gently but firmly swatting their posteriors.

"They may already have discovered us. It is only a matter of time. What do we have for defense and offense?"

"I have a gun, a few bullets, my knife, and a thousand Euros and a few dollars." Gloria says. "We can find a computer and disrupt their communications or learn what they plan, perhaps."

Anais says, "What do we need? I can still get a few resources, but my people may want conditions. I have a vehicle and money, but everywhere, the authorities are after me as a murderer."

"And you are such a gentle soul! Well, maybe we can make Laros come to us. Any ideas?"

Gloria in disguise enters an internet café somewhere in India. She orders a beverage and pays for internet access, surveys the people with her eyes shielded by shades and a scarf and then sits at a terminal.

As she works, men come into the café. They begin discretely to converge on her. She notices them and prepares to leave by force if necessary. Charles Nought enters and smiles at Gloria. He approaches her without apparent guile.

"Miss Brazed! How nice to catch up with you again. I assure you, I mean you no harm. Orr has requested your reinstatement. Please come with me and I will prove what I say."

Gloria pretends she is not the target of this conversation and considers running, but the escort of dangerous-looking men encircling her is too much.

"Nought, how could I possibly trust you, after you tried to kill me so many times?"

"Well, you are mistaken about me; I only act in the interests of the company, and only upon direct orders. Today my orders are to help you to rejoin the company and empower you to assist me in the investigation we have ongoing, contra Otoys. What do you say? Shall we go?"

Gloria allows herself to be escorted from the café, but she covertly sends a webcam message to Anais, including both pictures and the voices of the scene. Anais already has the address of Gloria's PDA.

Another private jet. This jet is more of a cargo craft than a luxury liner, yet it has comfortable lounge furniture and tables, some row seats, and an office-like area in the forward compartment.

Gloria enters, looking around for anything she might use to her advantage if she must fight. She remains calm, but she knows she is in danger.

The guards and Charles Nought enter.

"I see you still have a taste for knock-offs, my dear. Boris, would you relieve the lady of her purse?"

Boris and another man fight Gloria for the purse. They get damaged, but she is knocked down at last. Boris brings the purse to Nought.

While Gloria recovers, Nought uses her telephone camera to record the injuries on Gloria.

"Handy gadgets. I'll bet that John is in your phone book. I'll send him some entertainment. Boris, don't you think the lady is overdressed?"

Boris and another henchman restrain Gloria and tear her clothes while Nought takes photos.

"You are very attractive, my dear. You must use that advantage very well. Boris, would you please use that knife in her bag to trace a few light lines of red? She is too pale to photograph well."

Boris enjoys making Gloria bleed. Gloria will not show fear. She spits in Boris' face. He puts the knife to her nose and presses hard enough to let the blood start.

"That's enough for now, Boris. You can have more fun later. We'll send this collection of entertaining clips to John Ball, who will no doubt, attempt to rescue the little whore."

CHAPTER XVIII

TARGET

The colors of the cheap Indian hotel are bright, but the state of repair of the Seedy Hotel Lounge is depressing. There are noisy patrons and vendors shouting and haggling all around Anais and John. Anais hangs her head, overcome with sadness. John stares at her telephone video display with controlled rage.

John closes the camera. He looks around the room for enemies he could destroy. He forces relaxation into his manner.

"It is a trap."

"Of course it is a trap."

"Find that airplane. It is a 737 conversion. It is probably registered to a dummy, but it had to take off from somewhere or be in hangar somewhere."

"I will forward these pictures to the Yellow Group and they will help."

"Send them to RMS also. Orr is not the only person who will see them. I may still have a few friends."

John and Anais are disguised as they board an old DC-3. The night helps. The other passengers boarding are all Indian merchants, except for one oriental man, who studiously avoids looking at John and Anais.

"This will take a long time."

"If she is still alive, we will get her. If she has been killed, we will take care of that. We cannot control time."

"They sent more pictures. These are worse."

John and Anais enter the door of the airplane and the attendant begins to close the door, but a shout is heard and two men come running to board at the last minute. They look like European tourists, with backpacks for luggage. They board and the flight attendant closes the door. The plane begins to taxi.

In the noisy airplane, Anais sleeps on John's shoulder. He keeps alert, for anyone on the flight could be his next enemy. The tension is high when he catches the latecomers looking his way.

The next morning at the airport in Suva, Fiji, John and Anais are cleared through the customs. John has regained his composure. They hurry toward an automobile rental counter, closely followed by some of the other passengers on their flight. Anais does the negotiation. John turns to assess the people behind him. They stare at him. He smiles faintly. He turns to Anais and speaks so that everyone can hear him.

"I hope you got the fastest car they have, dear. I feel the need for speed."

Cars chase over Fijian roads, through sleepy villages, Jungles and farms, up into the mountains.

Then there are foot chases through jungles, more farm fields, through apartments, huts, churches, restaurants. The chase returns to the ocean.

There is an underwater chase past sharks, manta rays, barracudas, and among whales. Anais has good swimming form. John swims more like a turtle each moment.

A gang of locals chase the chasers and John and Anais because they are disturbing the police. The police are slow, so they mostly catch the chasers.

John and Anais swim cautiously up to a yacht ladder and climb on board.

John grins. "Yes, this looks familiar."

John calls out, "Captain Wayne! D'you be in want of a cook?"

Anais sits on the seat cushion, exhausted but posing as nicely as a model. John takes position beside the hatchway. Wayne and Dorothy come running up the stairs. John seizes Wayne in a control hold and kisses Dorothy on the cheek.

"My god, man! Is it you?"

"In the flesh, chum! Hello Dorothy, it is truly delightful to find you both well and happy!"

"You're both dripping. Let me get you towels. Hello, dear, I'm Dorothy. John, where is Gloria?"

"I'm Anais, Dorothy. I've heard so much about you. Gloria is in trouble. That's why we are here."

Wayne greets Anais as if she will be his next girlfriend. Then he gets some beers out of a cooler beneath the seat cushions. Dorothy gets towels and playfully rubs John's hair.

"We need a favor, you see."

"Anything. What's mine is yours, John boy. You need not even ask. What's the trouble?"

Anais says, "Gloria has been kidnapped. She is being tortured in Tonga."

"That's terrible! We must go rescue her immediately! Wayne!"

"It will probably be dangerous. It will also cost some money, and we haven't anything but the clothes on our backs."

"We can be in Nuku'alofa day after tomorrow. Get whatever you need, or rather, I will, and rest easy. If we can do anything for you and Gloria, we will. And you can rely on our crew, too. After that problem we had, I got really picky about who we have on board."

John and Anais relax at last, feeling momentarily safe.

On the Nuku'alofa customs wharf, a Tongan official studies the tourists and their papers. His men search the ship. There are onlookers at the wharf who seem suspicious. At last the official allows the four to pass. Wayne shakes the official's hand and passes some money to the man. A welcome band is playing loud music.

"Let's have a drink, John. I happen to know a local barman who may be of some use."

Wayne, Dorothy, John and Anais enter a Tongan bar and are greeted warmly by Marcus, the owner.

"Welcome, welcome again to my house, captain! Please allow me to bring you whatever you desire!"

All parties shake hands and sit. Wayne leans close to Marcus and winks.

"We are on a hunt, my friend, and we may need some equipment and a guide."

"Good my friend, you know the King does not allow hunting in Tonga! Fishing is another thing! You wish to go fishing!"

"Someone allowed the sharks to bring a pretty sailfish here and they are tearing her to pieces. We must rescue her."

"I think I know these sharks. They like the cliffs of Houma. Danger in that water. Many boats sink there."

A man in the bar rises and leaves. Anais studies him.

"These sharks have pilot fish. I recognize that man."

"Do not worry. I will take you to the place where the sharks are, and I have some equipment you may use, too."

Marcus drives a tiny jeep through the pitch-black night before moon-rise. The jeep also contains John and Anais and a bag. He stops. They listen and then they get out quietly.

"This is as close as we can be. These men, they have cameras and other things to know you are coming. They made a security system for the palace, and the King let them have this place. Now no one can come here."

John looks around for dangers. Anais scans with an electronic device.

"Nothing yet."

John motions to follow. He enters the jungle. Anais follows. Marcus stays with the vehicle. He has a pistol but he keeps it hidden. He produces a large banana and proceeds to eat it slowly. He hears a sound of boots approaching but he pretends he doesn't care.

John and Anais pause in the jungle with a moonrise view of a block house on the edge of the cliffs. One vehicle, a local jeep, is parked next to the building.

"I've got a hum."

Suddenly men jump on them. In a blur of action, they fight and begin running through the jungle. John breaks the neck of one assailant and Anais knocks out another. A third one escapes. John and Anais see that both attackers were oriental.

"Not mine."

"They don't belong to Nought. Well, let's see if the commotion made waves."

They move back toward the block house. Now there are many men around the building.

"I can draw them into the jungle while you go get her."

John looks at Anais with concern.

"Do you have friends there?"

Anais looks sad but determined.

"I seem to have lost all my friends. You don't trust me anymore."

John grins.

"I wouldn't want to be taken for granted."

Suddenly their attention is drawn to the house and guards. Some of the guards are running toward the jungle and some toward the edge of the cliffs.

"We have competition. Come on, you're off the hook for now."

They use whatever cover is available. They encounter guards and defeat them, but just as they almost reach the blockhouse they are surrounded by a mixed group of guards and assassins. John is enveloped in assassins and is dragged away unconscious. Anais is also wrapped in battle, but she escapes in another direction.

John Ball is tied to a chair. The room is non-descript and dark. Six black-clad small men all wearing hoods stand waiting.

John wakens, tries to move but cannot. He looks around at his captors with an amused smirk on his face.

John addresses the assassins in Cantonese. "I believe I have met some of your fathers. Their legitimate sons are much taller."

A door opens and another black-clad assassin enters. He dials a number on a satellite telephone.

"I appreciate that. I wanted to make a call."

The head assassin places the telephone so that John may talk.

Laros Opecoe is on the phone. "Hello. Who is this? How did you get this number?"

"Laros! This is John Ball. We still haven't had that talk and walk."

The Head Assassin takes the telephone away and listens.

"Mr. Ball! I thought you were dead! Where in the world are you?"

The Head Assassin says, "He is in our hands. We have decided to deliver him to you on one condition."

The Head Assassin holds the phone away from his ear while Laros fulminates, and then Head Assassin gives directions.

"You will bring ten million pounds to a place we specify in two hours and then we will deliver Ball to you. If not, then we have another customer."

John silently laughs at the thought that he is worth so much to Opecoe.

"Only ten million! Surely more!"

The Head Assassin closes the phone. He strikes John on the sternum.

"You are worth nothing. Better hope that Opecoe pays for you!"

"I suppose the tong would not pay you at all?"

The Head Assassin grins.

"Try more hard, Mister Ball!"

"Then you don't want the money, you want Laros Opecoe himself! Why?"

"Ten thousand cuts, Mr. Ball! He deserves that!"

"Well, I couldn't agree with you more. Let me go, and I will make sure he pays for what he has done."

"Your methods are too gentle, Mr. Ball."

"My mother taught me to be a gentleman."

Shots are heard. The Head Assassin and four others go out to fight. One assassin guards the door, and one comes to John. He looks angry. Shots and screams continue from outside.

"What did you do with Anais Ikk?"

"We had a few laughs."

"No joke. Must know what happened to leader."

John realizes that this fellow is one of the "Yellow Group."

"She was fighting alongside when you fellows knocked me out. I am sorry, I don't know. I hope she did not suffer the same fate as my dear Kiri."

The attackers burst into the room and shoot the Chinese assassins. They untie John but they do not free him. Instead they blindfold him and tie him to an elbow bar with tape. Then they force him to walk out with them.

CHAPTER XIX

QUESTIONING

This is the same mostly-cargo, part-human transport private jet plane interior in which Gloria was tortured.

The captors take the blindfold off of John. He is restrained to a gurney with leather and chain and buckles.

"This looks familiar. Do you serve champagne on this flight?"

The muscle-bound, business-suited henchmen all laugh.

"Make all the jokes you want, Mister Ball. Soon you will be laughing out of the other side of your mouth." The Head Henchman replies.

John glances around and tries his bindings.

"You've gone to a lot of trouble on my account. Is all this quite necessary? I mean, where could I run to?"

"Never mind asking. You have some hurting coming to you, and we don't care whether you are comfy or not, Buster."

"I do despise that name. Please call me John."

The Head Henchman takes a lead-filled bag with a handle from his pocket.

"Know what this is? It's lights out!"

The Head Henchman hits John with the sapper. John loses consciousness. The henchmen laugh like a chorus.

John awakens in a tile-walled room with only one skinny window, through which he hears a Muezzin calling. Men in brown caftans are in the room, seated on a tile bench. John is naked and strapped to a metal gurney.

"I thought you boys were from Otoys."

The men in brown caftans laugh. Some of them are the henchmen from the plane, and some of them are new and more obviously of Middle Eastern origin.

„Salaam Aleichem."

„Aleichem Salaam." the Henchmen reply.

The questioner approaches John and makes a short prayer in Arabic accented by Egyptian.

"Merciful Allah, if it be your will, let this heathen endure for a thousand years of questioning, and may his eyes be open when he dies, so that he may see the glorious peace of Allah, the merciful."

The questioner chooses a small whip with many lashes on it.

"Have you anything to tell us, John Ball?"

"Inshallah."

The questioner begins to apply the whip.

John endures as well as possible a long torture, including water boarding, nail pulling, burning with straw, cigarettes, iron, and also chemicals, and electric shocks and flesh hooks and salt in wounds and hot pepper dust in throat, eyes, and nose. Throughout the ordeal, the henchmen never ask anything, but they laugh at every sound of pain made by John.

At last they unbind him and sew him into a rough hemp sack. They toss his limp body onto a cart and pull the cart through a dark hallway to wooden doors which open to a street, where a van waits. They throw the sack into the back of the van and shut the doors. Then they all cheer in Arabic.

"His fate has been sealed by the will of merciful Allah!" Then they make the music of ulululation.

The driver and another man throw the sack containing John into the water of the Nile Delta. Then they slap the water with sticks and reeds to call the crocodiles. Bright splinters of sunlight ricochet from the broken water.

The crocodiles gape their mouths and roar when they hear the call. Some begin swimming toward the disturbance.

John rips the sack open and struggles to the surface just as a large crocodile closes on him.

The henchmen watch the water roil. Some crocodiles come out of the water and move toward the henchmen. The men get in the van and drive away.

John has got his arms and legs around an enormous crocodile and is stroking its belly to hypnotize it. The crocodile goes into a passive trance with John on its back.

"Dundee didn't do this!"

John starts the crocodile waving his tail and that automatic response propels them through the water away from the other crocodiles.

At the mouth of the Nile John points the crocodile toward a group of ducks and slips off the unwitting transport. The crocodile awakens and moves toward the ducks. John swims toward the Mediterranean. Day becomes night.

The fisherman has a lantern on a pole which attracts fish. He then catches fish in his net. John comes to the boat from the dark side. He pulls himself up part-way. The fisherman turns and is startled. He addresses John in Coptic, and John responds in Coptic.

"Brother, you are in need?"

"Will you take a poor man on board?"

"Yes, brother. Where is your boat?"

"At the bottom of the sea. Thank you for your hospitality."

John is helped to come on board by the fisherman. He is smoking a cigarette. He hands the cigarette to John, who nods and takes a puff. The fisherman points to the leeches which cover John.

"Use fire on the leeches. I will make a taper. You must have swum a long way."

"I was thrown into the delta by some men who tortured me because I was not of their faith. I rode a crocodile to the mouth, by the grace of God, and I swam to your boat. I thank you for being here."

"Brother, I would not be here if I had caught enough fish. I cannot go home until I have caught something to sell, to feed my family."

John throws off the last of the bloody leeches and smiles at the Fisherman.

"Then let us catch a wonderful fish, so that you may return proud with a full purse."

John takes the oars and pulls, because he sees by the starlight a group of rocks barely protruding from the waves a hundred feet from shore.

"Have you caught anything here before?"

"Yes, but it got away from me. Perhaps it still lives here. I need a line strong enough for a big fish and a hook as large as your hand."

The fisherman produces such a hook and line and puts a bait fish on the hook. He hands the hook and line to John. Then the fisherman gets his pole with three hooked points.

"I know this fish. I have tried to catch him many times. He is very strong. It will take both of us to bring him in."

John slips into the water with the hook. He ties the line to the boat. He dives at the edge of the light down to the lair of the fish.

John pulls the bait fish across the entrance of the cave where the big fish likes to hang out. The big fish takes the bait. John sets the hook. He begins swimming up, pulling the line attached to the boat. The big fish tries to shake the hook, but cannot. He swims out of the cave and attempts to escape in the open water.

John surfaces and grabs the boat just as the big fish begins to tow the boat. He climbs in. The boat picks up speed.

"That was good fishing, brother. What is your name?"

"I am called John."

They let the fish pull them until it is tired. Then the Fisherman uses his gaff hook..John uses the net rope. They pull the ancient fish into the boat. It flops. It almost fills the boat.

John and the fisherman row up to the landing and tie onto a rock. They get the enormous fish out of the boat and begin to carry it to the market, to the applause and cheers of all the onlookers.

John makes a call to a friend at RMS from a telephone booth in the Egyptian fish market.

"Larry, can you help me without letting Nought know I am here? No, he's a double agent, and he has tried to kill me and my minder several times already. No, I'm not out of my mind. Yes, I would appreciate that. I'm not so sure whether Orr might be in on the plot also."

John hears a mysterious sound on the line.

"Bye for now darling, I'll be in touch when my ship is ready to sail."

The crowd of men in the Egyptian tea parlor is mixed. Some are in western business attire, some are in traditional garb. John is in worn clothes bought in a used-clothing booth, and wears a rag turban.

Two men enter and see John. They approach his table and salute him in oriental fashion.

"May we join you, Mr. Ball? I am called Minkus and this gentleman is Armin."

"Please have a cup of tea with me. How do you know me?"

"Our company knows everything. We know you have returned from the dead, and that you have called for help, and that you do not trust your employer to provide that help."

"Yeah, well, their track record is spotty. What do you want?"

"Whom do you trust, Mr. Ball?"

"No one comes to mind."

"We have the same problem. What is your impression of Opecoe?"

"Animal. Not mineral or vegetable. Terminally evil, but unproven as far as direct culpability goes."

Armin says, "We are a more reliable employer, Mr. Ball. Would you please come with us?"

"Not willingly."

John is hit from behind with a sapper. He slumps forward.

"As you wish."

Armin and Minkus lift John and walk him out, followed by the Sapper wielder. None of the men in the tea shop seem to notice.

Minkus splashes John with a liquid which wakes him and disgusts him at the same time. They are in the caves of AndoSys, to judge by the logo carved into the cave wall.

"I asked for champagne, not vinegar."

He tries to rise and discovers he is bound to a chair again.

"We are going to have some fun, Buster." Minkus says.

"Look, I've already had the finest treatment that the Browns and Otoys could provide and I haven't had a good laugh yet. As far as I am concerned, Laros is a bad guy with a good tailor, and Hammerman and Guntzee and Hammadegi should have a meeting with a vest bomber. Do you know a slut who will do the job?"

"You will, Mr. Ball. You are an assassin slut. We will pay you, or we will force you. It is up to you." Armin smiles.

"I'm all business. Now, could we dispense with the ritual torture?"

"But that is the fun part, Buster."

"That name is a deal-breaker, Minky. Call me John, or don't call me."

"I'm so glad you said that, Buster. Now I will have my fun."

Minkus produces an electric shock device and applies it to John Ball.

A convoy of limousines and SUV's works its way through a crowd of beggars on a street in Tunis outside a factory. Among the beggars is John Ball in disguise. John forces his way to an automobile window and shows his face to the occupants. The limousine halts. Laros Opecoe opens the door and steps out. He throws coins to the crowd. John confronts him, leaning close to speak among the noises of the crowd.

"John! What a surprise! Please come with us, and I will make amends."

John empties a syringe of something green into Opecoe's left arm.

"That's all right. I've always been an outcast. Have fun in hell, Laros".

Laros Opecoe is paralyzed and dying, but he seems only to be thinking about what to say. John shakes his hand and melts into the crowd of beggars.

A guard says, "Mr. O, let's go! I don't like the look of this crowd!"

When Laros does not respond, the guards beat back the beggars and rush to find that Opecoe is dead. They toss him into the auto and speed away, knocking down and running over beggars in their path.

"You are even bad when you are dead, Laros."

John is once more dressed well. He wears stylish dark glasses which he removes as he enters the dark and gilded Majestic Bar. He takes a stool where he may observe the comings and goings. The bartender approaches.

"Stout, please. Have you sent the message?"

Anais, in a concealing scarf, slides into a position behind John.

"Message received, darling."

John breathes in her perfume with pleasure.

"Narcissus and Myrrh! Somewhat tawdry, my dear."

John turns to see her.

"Is it not welcome?"

"On the contrary. Welcome as an early spring after a glacial winter. I had confidence you would still be kicking."

The bartender places two beverages on the counter.

"When I heard about Laros, I knew you would be here. Are we on holiday?"

John tastes his beer. Anais flirts with her half-hidden eyes.

"I am all business, Anais. I have old debts to pay in Cairo and some accounting must be done in Dublin."

"We have a friend who still needs help. She is in Cairo. One of my group is there."

John is both startled and pleased at this news. However, he suspects a trap.

"She is still the bait, and it is still a trap. Did you get questioned as gently as they grilled me?"

"I am dying to show you the scars, dear. I bruise as easily as you."

John finishes his beer, rises and offers his arm to Anais.

"Then you will need some TLC before we journey on."

John and Anais lean against the rail of a cruise ship. They are watching the port of Alexandria come closer.

"We will take the fast train into Cairo, and the Metro to the Faiyoum, where the Browns have an office building. Where do you think they have Gloria?"

"They put her in a hotel, the Wali Sayed. I think one of the ministers owns it. They will have it ready for our attempt."

"Perhaps we can make them move her. I am an amateur pyromaniac."

Fire trucks and sirens and commotion and vehicles racing from the building are a background to John and Anais on motorcycles.

John and Anais chase the limos to the edges of the Souk, where a large truck blocks their path. Men with guns come out of the vehicles and begin shooting at John and Anais.

The Yellow Group mole and another man, a Brown, drag Gloria out of a car which has been disabled, toward another car. Gloria lashes out and is helped by the Yellow group mole to down the Brown Guard. They run. John and Anais pick them up and go into the narrow pathways of the Souk. The Yellow Group Mole is shot by the pursuers and falls off Anais' bike.

At the other end of the Souk, they find more vehicles waiting. A train begins to move next to the Souk. John and Anais, with Gloria riding behind John, go up some outside stairs, across a roof, up a board ramp, through the air and land on top of a sleeper car of the train. The train has just reached a fair speed. The vehicles full of gunmen follow, shooting at the train. The train begins to stop. John and Anais gun their motorbikes and vault from the train to a gravel siding. Anais falls. John stops to help. Anais has a broken arm. Gloria drives the bike with Anais riding behind her.

Cars chase them after getting around the train. Many shots are fired. John finally finds a way through tangled narrow slum streets and loses the pursuit at the edge of a slum. He stops to celebrate, but Anais has been shot. She is dying in his arms.

"Promise me, John. Destroy the Brown..."

Gloria holds Anais also, and her tears fall on Anais' face.

"I promise."

John and Gloria are disguised as American tourists in flower-print shirts and shorts and sandals and straw hats. They clear customs in Cyprus with no problem.

In the lobby are men who follow John and Gloria. Nought is seen leaning casually against a display. He waves at the travelers.

John walks up to Nought as if he is a long-lost friend and offers his hand.

While John is demonstratively shaking Nought's hand, Gloria takes Nought's gun and knife and wallet and passports. John continues holding on to Nought, forcing him to come along because of an especially painful pincer grip on a nerve.

John, Gloria and Nought get into a taxi. Gloria taps the driver on the shoulder.

"We want to see the countryside. Are you available for all day? We will pay you three hundred Euros."

The taxi driver smiles and nods. Gloria drops some bills onto the front seat. She counts Nought's money. The taxi driver pulls out into the road. Other cars pull out also.

"Thank you for meeting us at the airport, Charles."

"You won't get away with this, Buster!"

"I'm sure we would get along better if you did not call me that, Charles. What other toys have you brought us?"

John pats Charles' pockets discretely, finding and removing some miniature grenades and another knife. He finds another Otoys recording device and tosses it out the window.

"Orr knows you have defected to the AndoSys and the Yellows. You are both on the 'seek and destroy' list. I tried to save you, but you would not cooperate."

"Save us for what? Which groups are you working for?" Gloria demands.

"I have been on assignment to dis-inform the opposition. You couldn't understand."

Gloria points to the scars on her face and neck and elsewhere generally, although they are covered by clothes.

"Oh, I understand, Charles Nought! I understand."

One of the pursuing vehicles pulls alongside and a man with a gun aims at John. He shoots. The bullet nicks Nought's ear and breaks glass but does not hit John.

The taxi driver curses in Greek and in Turkish.

Gloria shoots back and the pursuit vehicle falls behind.

"Taxi driver, two hundred Euros more if you can lose that car! They are bandits!"

The taxi speeds. The roads are twisting and narrow, going up and down hills and around mountains and across dry stream beds. For a moment they lose the followers.

"Driver! Stop!"

The taxi slides to a stop above a steep decline. John forces Nought to get out and cuts his shoelaces.

"It has been so nice to see you again, Charles. I'm sure your friends will give you a lift."

John gets back into the taxi.

"Driver, can we go back and take another road?"

They drive to one of the many gravel and caliche road forks and see the dust of the pursuit to the left, so they take the fork to the right, which leads away from Charles' location.

"This is fun! Taxi driver man, are you having fun?"

The driver looks over his shoulder at the woman with the gun. He grins in a most uncertain way.

On the back roads of Cyprus there is a chase over the roads, through the villages, up into the mountainous interior of Cyprus. Bullets and chickens fly, ladders fall, dust clouds envelop action. The magnificent views are obscured.

"Well, we have lost two of the other team. Shall we go fishing, or get some supper?"

"I haven't worked up an appetite yet."

Just then a helicopter rises up from a low place and faces them. The men in the helicopter fire automatic weapons at the cab, hitting the radiator and other places. John, Gloria and the driver pile out of the taxi just before it blows up.

"Come on! There's a cave!" John says.

While the cloud of smoke and fire gives them cover, they run into the cave.

The taxi driver stops in fear. The Cave is more terrible to him than the bullets.

"No! This is the cave of the old gods! My taxi! My taxi!"

He pulls his hair and beats his fists on his chest.

"Here. The company will pay for it. They won't shoot at you. It is us they want."

John hands the card of Charles Nought to the taxi driver.

"Wasn't that fun? Here, I only have a thousand Euros. You can have it. Okay?" Gloria smiles at the Taxi Driver, and he stops wailing.

The taxi driver is calmed by the money. He looks out of the cave. The helicopter has moved away. He looks back fearfully into the cave.

"Yes, it was fun! Goodbye! Have some more fun! If you come to my house, we will have coffee and Spanakopita and…"

He is running out of the cave while he is talking.

"Gloria, alone at last! Do you have any regrets?"

"Regrets are for declining boring parties, John; I haven't been bored yet today. Are you about to bore me?"

The helicopter appears in view and a pursuit vehicle drives slowly up the road toward the burning taxi.

"I try to be a stimulating guest. Shall we take a tour?"

They climb into the cave, away from the entrance.

By the glow of a key-chain light, they slog through guano and insects. Gloria is disgusted and gagging. John gives her a handkerchief to cover her nose and mouth.

"You seem to have a penchant for nasty holes."

"This is bat guano, not human waste. Much more dangerous and interesting because of histoplasmosis, you see."

Gloria slips into a deeper pile and loses her footing. She is covered in muck.

"I seem to be having more fun than you. Wouldn't you like to share what fun I just had?"

John turns off the light. There is a faint glow ahead of them and there are noises behind them.

"Come on. I smell fresh air."

"I don't know how you could smell anything but this bat crap. Even Lagerfeld would be an improvement."

They struggle toward a shaft of light.

John crawls out of the small hole in the mountain and helps Gloria to come out also. They are covered in awful goo and their clothes are shredded. There is a nice view of the ocean.

"Look. Our spa awaits us."

He points toward a pool and spring with an ancient priapic column beside it.

"I can guess which god this belongs to."

They see no helicopter or cars, no opposition, so they climb down to the pool, throw off their clothes and plunge into the water as if they were care-free. Gloria splashes water on John, and John splashes her in return.

The helicopter finds the bathers and men begin shooting toward the pool. The bathers run to cover beneath the trees. The helicopter moves closer, searching. A flash is seen from the ground. Metal grinds, the helicopter blades slow and fold and the aircraft falls.

John and Gloria are crouched naked among the rocks and trees. Gloria holds the pistol, grins, raises the muzzle and blows the smoke away.

"Excellent shot, darling. You get the gold laurel wreath."

The helicopter crashes and explodes.

"You look like a Greek hero, John."

"We are not overdressed for heroes this time, Glory. We might want to find some fig leaves."

John and Gloria, in their torn but scrubbed clothes, walk down the street toward a taverna in a Greek fishing village holding hands. The early evening is bright and clear, with a full moon rising and gentle breezes making Gloria's hair wave and dance.

"We can be cooks again. We will find a way. I wish Anais and Kiri could be here on such a fine night."

Gloria hugs John. He pauses and gives her a kiss, then pulls her toward the taverna.

"Come on. I fear you might be getting bored."

"I'll let you know. When I get bored, you will fear me."

John and Gloria enter with smiles on their faces and rags on their bodies. They take a table. John grins at all the sailors and fishermen in the crowded room.

"We had a little mishap and sank!" He speaks like a local.

He pulls out some money.

"Drinks for all, to celebrate our good luck!"

The mood of the crowd improves. Each man comes to offer condolences and advice. One man stares at them.

"You don't remember me?"

John studies the man. Gloria puts her hand on her pistol, inside her pull-over pocket.

"We may have met one time in Africa."

The man raises his arms in a display of appreciation.

"Goal! Yes, I am Rogier. You saved us from the pirates!"

John and Gloria recognize the man at last.

"You look much nicer now, Rogier."

He beams with pride and sits down with them.

"I should look better with a hundred pounds of good food under my belt and a new wife!"

The waitress brings food and wine. John looks quizzically at the waitress. She smiles seductively at Rogier.

"We have not yet ordered anything."

"You will never have to order anything while you are around us! Eat! Drink! Enjoy!"

John, Gloria, Rogier and Rogier's wife are on a yacht, entering a Romanian harbor. The moonlight is strong and clear.

"I wish you would just hang out with us and let me take care of you." Rogier says.

"Nothing would be more pleasant, Rogier. When we finish our business, we may take you up on your offer."

John walks in to a minister's office. The minister calls for protection. Guns are drawn by plain-clothes guards. John produces a disc player. When the minister sees what is on it, he offers money. John turns away. Uniformed officers come in and arrest the minister as John walks away.

On the Orient Express, John and Gloria are surprised as they enter the club car by two men wearing brown jackets. After a brief tussle both men are down. John drags them out one by one, throwing them from the train. He then straightens his clothes and rejoins Gloria, who has ordered drinks and is being served by a waiter.

"Now we have begun the evening exercise. Have you worked up an appetite yet?"

"Just a little thirst. Notice the dregs in the bottle of this wine, dear."

The steward realizes he has been discovered. He pulls out a knife, but John breaks the man's windpipe with a swift blow. The man grabs his throat and drops the knife. Gloria pushes him out the door and off the train.

"I know it was your turn, dear, I apologize. You may have the next steward."

Gloria and John join a tour of the Dax exchange and watch as the price of Otoys plummets and trade is halted. Someone points them out to a guard. They leave to evade interrogation.

In Spain, Gloria gives a gift box to a ragged street urchin, who runs away to brag.

"Well, that's the last of the money from short-selling Otoys."

A van full of Guardia Civil pulls to a halt. The soldier-police pile out. John and Gloria go running. The police blow their whistles and fire their guns, but John and Gloria are not hit.

In a Moroccan fishing village John is repairing fishing net. He squats on the beach with the ancient fisherman who owns the boat. Gloria, wearing a local costume, with her face and hair covered, brings food to the men. Other men in small groups are arranged down the beach, doing similar chores.

An inflatable boat with four men comes toward the shore. They begin firing automatic rifles at the fishermen. The old man falls. John and Gloria get behind the boat and fire back. By the time they have killed the attackers; several more fishermen have been shot.

"This has got to stop." Gloria cries for the fishermen and their families.

"I quite agree."

"How, then?"

"Only one way, my dear."

"Well, okay, let's go do it."

They gather a few things and walk into the surf. Fisher families are wailing over their dead and injured. John and Gloria toss the bodies of the assailants overboard and leave on the inflatable boat.

John and Gloria are dressed in local clothes, exiting a microbus in Tenerife with other workers. They enter an office building with the janitorial staff; the logo on the outside is AndoSys.

John and Gloria plant bombs in the Server room. They gather their mops and buckets and exit the building. They walk with other workers in similar clothes down the street and into a hotel. The bombs explode behind them, and the AndoSys building tumbles down.

John and Gloria are at the hotel bar, dressed in their British tourist clothes. The other tourists around them are quite nervous. An embassy official enters the hotel lobby. He proceeds to the bar and claps twice for attention.

"As you know, terrorists have struck again. Several different groups have claimed responsibility. They appear to be targeting British and Americans as usual. Therefore, as a precaution, we have arranged to evacuate anyone who wishes, to safety. The autobus is waiting outside and will depart in ten minutes for the airport. Please have your passports ready for inspection."

The crowd of tourists scrambles and goes to get their luggage. John finishes his drink.

"Shall we?"

CHAPTER XX

MASTER

John and Gloria look quite smart as they enter an elevator in the lobby of BHC with RMS displayed on the reader board.. Six tall and dangerous men crowd into the elevator with them.

Elevator doors open. John and Gloria step out. Incapacitated men cover the floor of the elevator behind them.

"Mr. Orr and Mr. Nought are expecting you. Please go right in." The receptionist intones.

John gives a fetching smile to the receptionist. She blushes beet red and her mouth parts to show wet lips and brilliantly white teeth.

"Thank you. Thank you very much."

Gloria stops and turns to face him.

"You know I would go to the ends of the earth for you, darling?"

"Haven't we already done that?"

"Don't be a bore, this once."

John smiles and shrugs. He nods toward the golden door of Orr. Gloria turns and they both proceed through the door, which opens automatically and shuts silently behind them.

"Welcome, and bravo! Well done! I say, your performance contra both Otoys and AndoSys was remarkable! I had learned of the collusion of the Brown Group with AndoSys, and had hoped you would be bright enough to take care of the problem."

John gives a slight nod.

"I am gratified that you approve. I thought…"

"Oh, I don't approve of your methods, Ball. But the results partially redeem you. Still, there seems to be some problem right here in our midst, which you may be able to explain to me."

Gloria pulls a disc from her clutch.

"This data, compiled from AndoSys files and from Otoys and Brown Group files, will explain it to you, Sir."

Orr looks as if he does not want to accept it,

"Well, what does it show? Buster, do you know about this disc?"

"I can vouch for the authenticity and content completely, sir."

"The disc details the evil practices of Opecoe, the conspiracy to monopolize much of world trade for political advantage, and the total duplicity of the double agent, Charles Nought."

Orr looks displeased. Nought emerges from a niche.

"Yes, I thought you might say that. Charles has told me all about your defection, your misalliances under duress, and your false accusations."

Nought puts on a serious comradely smile for Orr's benefit.

"They are both double agents. It is only a coincidence that Laros has fallen and AndoSys has been reformed without the Browns."

Orr waves his hands as if to dismiss petty squabbles among his children.

"Now, can't we all just get along for a change?"

"I need a drink."

Charles maneuvers toward the bar at the same time as John.

"May I fix a drink for you, Charles? It will be like old times."

Orr assumes a fatherly mode.

"Shan't we all have a drink? Bygones! A toast to our success, no matter how it has been accomplished!"

"John has kept his gaze upon Charles, and he does so even whilst pouring the drinks and handing them to the others.

"Success, then!"

They toast and sip. Orr smiles paternally. Gloria drops her glass and falls to the floor dead.

"Glory!" John cries out.

Orr looks at Gloria in horror. He puts his glass down and backs away. John kneels, holds Gloria in his arms and sheds a tear.

"Ball has murdered her!"

Nought pulls out a gun to shoot John. John gets off the first shot, killing Nought. Nought looks surprised and falls backwards.

"I don't know how you did it, Charles. It was not me. Bon voyage to nothingness, Nought!"

Orr is afraid for his own life.

"My god! What have you done?"

John puts the disc in a computer slot and points to the monitor.

"You will see. Study that. Nought was the double, or rather, triple agent. You slept with the viper. Nought chased us and tried to kill us all over the world. He claimed he was doing it on your orders. He did not want you to see this."

Orr gathers himself, watches the monitor for a moment, considers his options, and resumes his directorial voice.

"You simply cannot behave like this, Buster. I am thoroughly displeased. How can I trust anyone?"

John finishes his drink.

"Perhaps you'll get me killed next time. Would that make you happy?"

John kneels, picks up Gloria's hand and kisses it tenderly, briefly. Then he turns to walk out of the room.

"Stop right there, Buster! I won't hear of you being killed, so long as you bring me good information, and take care of problems efficiently. I did reinstate you, with a small bonus, for good results."

John turns to appraise Orr. He seems about to throw away the job, with a sneer of disgust rising on his face.

"Here now, I've chosen a new minder for you, Buster. Do take better care of her than you did of the late Miss Brazed!"

John turns again to see the new person. Orr steps forward to do the introduction, but maintains his professional distance.

"This is Miry Wan, John Ball."

(Harrumph)

I do hope you two get along. Now go along."

John and Miry exchange knowing glances.

"You look thirsty, my dear. How about a drink?"

John offers his arm to her.

"I hope you are a match to your sister."

"More than a match, Buster. You'll see."

John grins at the challenge. They exit through the padded, gilt leather automatic doors of Orr's office.

"Call me John."

THE END of OTOYS.

John Ball *RMS* will return in 'Gold Coast'